A DUKE'S LESSON IN CHARM

SOPHIE BARNES

A DUKE'S LESSON IN CHARM

The Gentlemen Authors

Cover Design by The Killion Group, Inc.

ALSO BY SOPHIE BARNES

Novels

The Gentlemen Authors

A Duke's Lesson In Charm

A Duke's Introduction To Courtship

A Duke's Guide To Romance

Brazen Beauties

Mr. West and The Widow

Mr. Grier and The Governess

Mr. Dale and The Divorcée

Diamonds in the Rough

The Dishonored Viscount

Her Scottish Scoundrel

The Formidable Earl

The Forgotten Duke

The Infamous Duchess

The Illegitimate Duke

The Duke of Her Desire

A Most Unlikely Duke

The Crawfords

Her Seafaring Scoundrel

More Than a Rogue

No Ordinary Duke

Secrets at Thorncliff Manor

Christmas at Thorncliff Manor

His Scandalous Kiss

The Earl's Complete Surrender

Lady Sarah's Sinful Desires

At The Kingsborough Ball

The Danger in Tempting an Earl

The Scandal in Kissing an Heir

The Trouble with Being a Duke

The Summersbys

The Secret Life of Lady Lucinda

There's Something About Lady Mary

Lady Alexandra's Excellent Adventure

Standalone Titles

The Girl Who Stepped Into The Past

How Miss Rutherford Got Her Groove Back

Novellas

Diamonds in the Rough

The Roguish Baron

The Enterprising Scoundrels

Mr. Clarke's Deepest Desire

Mr. Donahue's Total Surrender

The Townsbridges

An Unexpected Temptation

A Duke for Miss Townsbridge

Falling for Mr. Townsbridge

Lady Abigail's Perfect Match

When Love Leads To Scandal

Once Upon a Townsbridge Story

The Honorable Scoundrels

The Duke Who Came To Town

The Earl Who Loved Her

The Governess Who Captured His Heart

Standalone Titles

Only the Valet Will Do

Sealed with a Yuletide Kiss (An historical romance advent calendar)

The Secrets of Colchester Hall

Mistletoe Magic (from Five Golden Rings: A Christmas

Collection)

Miss Compton's Christmas Romance

CHAPTER ONE

London, October 1817

Callum Davis, Duke of Stratton, admired the book on his parlor table. After months of blood, sweat, and a few tears, the novel he and his friends, Anthony Gibbs, the Duke of Westcliffe and Brody Evans, the Duke of Corwin, had written together, was in front of him. Published. Ready for sale.

Printed with the assistance of Brody's wife, Harriet, and expertly bound by Anthony's wife, Ada, it truly was a joint effort. It was a wonderful day, despite the rain, and it was time for them to celebrate their achievement together.

"Can you believe we actually did it?" Brody asked

while Callum poured them each a glass of champagne. He glanced at Brody in time to see him pick up *Seductive Scandal* and turn it over between his hands. "I'm still in awe."

"It does feel a bit like a dream," Anthony said. "Just imagine all the people who will read it and all the homes it will fill."

"It's exciting," Callum said. He began distributing the glasses. "And terrifying."

"You've nothing to worry about," Ada said.

She'd been living above her uncle's bookshop when she and Anthony met. It was she who'd sparked the idea of the three men writing a romance novel in order to improve their incomes.

Like Anthony and Brody, Callum had wasted most of his fortune on various amusements as a means by which to distract himself from the loss of his father. He'd not been ready to go on without him. Papa hadn't been an old man. He should have lived several decades more and probably would have, had it not been for the accident that killed not only him but Anthony's and Brody's fathers as well.

A tragic occurrence, caused by an explosion inside a barn.

Callum tightened his hold on his glass and tried not to think of that awful day. Instead, he chose to focus on what he and his friends had accomplished. It was no small thing. "To romance and the marvelous success we hope it provides."

"Hear, hear," the others replied.

"I hope it sells a million copies," Harriet said.

Ada smirked. "All of us do, although that would set something of a record. I'm thinking a thousand copies to start would be impressive."

"Can it be done?" Brody asked.

"Having written a romance novel with my three friends and seeing it printed and bound, I feel like anything's possible," Callum remarked. He sipped his champagne, then jutted his glass toward the others. "Your marriages are further proof."

Both men had married women who'd lacked dowries and connections. Brody had even believed his wife to be a young man when he first met her – until he'd discovered her true identity.

Ada smiled at her husband. "He's not wrong."

"I couldn't agree with you more," Anthony murmured, dropping a quick kiss to her cheek.

"All we need to do now is see you happily settled," Brody remarked, nodding at Callum.

Callum coughed. "Let's focus on the book, shall we."

"It *would* make dinner parties a great deal simpler," Harriet said. "Even numbers make for a far more harmonious table setting."

"The book, if you'll recall," Callum said, attempting to get their minds away from the idea of him following in their footsteps any time soon. "We probably ought to make some sort of plan to promote it."

"We could place advertisements in the papers," Brody suggested.

"I've also been toying with the idea of having a card dropped off at various homes the day it releases," Harriet said. "It could have the title and price on one side with a short story outline on the other."

"I like that," Callum said. He gestured for his friends to sit before lowering himself to one of the armchairs. "It might even suggest some of the bookshops that carry the book."

"There's another thing we can do," said Ada. "One of the biggest influences upon a book's success is a prominent review. I've asked The Lady Librarian if she'd be willing to write one and she has agreed."

"The Lady Librarian?" Brody's eyebrows rose. "Impressive."

Callum agreed. The Lady Librarian had to be the most famous book critic in London. Her reviews appeared in *The Mayfair Chronicle* every Sunday. He'd personally purchased a few lesser-known book titles on the basis of her recommendations.

"I've already provided her with a copy of the book," Ada said, "and she has assured me she will start on it as soon as she finishes reading two others."

"So then, the review will likely be ready in one

month's time, give or take?" Harriet asked with eager excitement.

"Yes. I believe it will be published the same week the book is released."

"Extraordinary." Callum was wildly impressed. "How did you even know whom to contact? I thought her identity to be a secret."

"It is," Ada said. She fiddled with a piece of lace on her skirt. "Few people know who she really is, but it just so happens she and I are good friends."

"Lucky us." Anthony grinned and raised his glass for another toast. "To *Seductive Scandal* being a smashing success."

"I'll drink to that," Callum said with a laugh. He downed the remainder of his champagne and went to collect the bottle so he could refill the glasses. Glancing toward the window, he saw the rain had ceased and the sun had broken through the clouds.

"Looks like the weather's cleared up," Anthony said when he and Ada prepared to leave. "Maybe we can walk home instead of taking the carriage."

"Mind if Peter and I join you?" Callum asked. He enjoyed a good afternoon walk and believed the exercise was good for his ten-year-old ward.

"Of course not." Anthony turned to Brody and Harriet. "What say you?"

"I'm afraid we're off to Hudson & Co." The printing press where Harriet still worked, much to the shock and dismay of the *ton*, was in the opposite direction of Westcliffe House. "Thank you for offering though. And for the drink."

They said their goodbyes and took their leave. Callum went to fetch Peter and then the four of them headed toward Berkley Square. The pavement was wet, sending up the occasional spray of water whenever their shoes struck a spot where moisture had gathered. Callum took a deep breath. The air was fresher now, perhaps a bit cooler as well.

"Mama always loved rainy days," Peter murmured, his comment piercing Callum's heart.

It was only a few months since Callum's cousin, along with his cousin's wife, had died in a fire. Lewis Davis had named Callum in his will, asking that he take responsibility for his son if the worst were to happen. Peter had spoken very little since coming to live with Callum, despite Cullum's efforts to try and help him with his grief.

So far, he feared he was doing a terrible job.

"I can understand why," Ada said. "There's really nothing better than sitting inside while raindrops drum on the windows. I'm rather fond of it myself. Especially since such days are perfect for reading. Do you enjoy reading, Peter?"

"Sometimes."

"What's the best book you've read?" Ada asked.

"*Gulliver's Travels*," Peter remarked. He went very quiet before saying, "Papa used to read me a chapter at night before bed."

Unsure of how to respond, yet knowing the gut-wrenching pain he himself had gone through as a fully grown man when his father had died, Callum drew Peter close to his side and hugged him. He didn't care who might see or if they thought public displays of affection were inappropriate. The only important thing right now was helping Peter through this difficult time as best as he could.

"We've got that book in the library," Callum said once he'd released Peter. "I'm happy to read it for you if you like."

"Thank you, but it won't be the same," Peter muttered.

Of course it wouldn't. "Perhaps a different book then. We can visit the bookshops together. I'm sure we can find something to strike your interest."

"*The Swiss Family Robinson* might be an option," Ada suggested. "Unless you already own a copy."

"I believe…" Callum frowned when he noted the woman approaching from the opposite end of the street. Damnation. It was she. The Earl of Rosemont's daughter, Lady Emily. He'd recognize that ginger hair anywhere, even if he could only spy a few stray curls from beneath the brim of her fashionable bonnet. "Come, let's cross to the other side."

"Oh, but I cannot do that," Ada said. "Not without greeting my friend."

Callum almost tripped. "You and Lady Emily know one another?"

"Indeed." She shot a surprised look in Callum's direction. "It would seem you do too."

Of course they knew each other. They moved in the same circle and were of a similar age. Naturally, they'd both been present at various engagements over the years. Ever since her debut.

"I sense a story here," Anthony said with a hint of amusement.

Callum stared straight ahead at the woman who'd been approaching at a steady pace until she'd spotted him. There was an awkward look about her now, as though she wished to turn on her heels and run, but couldn't because of Ada. A strained smile appeared on her face as she straightened her posture and continued toward them.

"Let's just say she and I do not get along," Callum told Anthony.

"Why on earth not?" Ada asked. "She's perfectly lovely."

If one enjoyed being reduced to an imbecile all the time since this was the effect Lady Emily had upon him. For some unknown reason, the universe seemed to have it in for him when he found himself in her presence. It didn't help that he invariably said the wrong thing in an effort to smooth things over.

"She hates me," Callum informed his friends.

"Really?" Anthony chuckled. "I'm surprised you never mentioned it before."

It wasn't the sort of thing he cared to speak of. In

fact, he preferred to forget every interaction he'd had with Lady Emily. Not reminisce over them with friends. He eyed Anthony while slowing his pace. "It wasn't worth talking about."

Anthony snorted and then he and Ada were greeting Lady Emily. Callum hung back together with Peter, only the boy had spotted something that Callum had missed. Lady Emily wasn't alone. She was walking a small fluffy dog. Not a poodle, but some other breed Callum wasn't familiar with.

Peter went straight for it, pressing past Anthony and Ada and dropping into a crouch so he could stroke the dog's fur.

Callum stepped forward. "Peter. You can't just—"

"It's quite all right," Lady Emily told him, smiling down at the boy. "Heidi loves attention. The more the better. Provided you do not mind, Lord Stratton."

He didn't miss the added firmness to her voice when she spoke his title. It drew his attention and put him on edge as she always did when their paths crossed. But when she raised her gaze to his, all he saw was endless green.

Swallowing, he did his best not to let it affect him. And yet, there was no denying the impact she had upon him. No doubt Lady Emily had been blessed with the loveliest eyes in the world, the prettiest features, and the most kissable mouth. He'd always thought so, and therein lay the problem.

When he'd seen her last, his pulse had started to race as it always did in her presence. They'd been at the Farthington's ball and had met in a hallway. An exchange had followed with both of them wishing to flee the other's company as fast as possible. She'd stepped past him, he'd turned, and had inadvertently stepped on the hem of her gown.

The next thing he knew, she was falling. And it had once again been his fault.

Honestly, if the woman thought him an arse, or simply bad luck, he'd not be surprised. The point was, it was best if they didn't interact since he clearly couldn't behave as expected when he was around her.

Heidi leapt up onto her hind legs and licked at Peter's face. The boy laughed and Callum's heart swelled until it became a painful ache in his chest. Nothing had made the lad happy thus far.

Callum had tried having Cook prepare all manner of sweets. They'd been met with the same disinterest as rides in the park, a trip to the theatre, and the various toys Callum had bought him.

It seemed obvious now that an animal might do what all other efforts had failed to accomplish.

"Where are you heading?" Ada asked Lady Emily.

"To the park. I've been praying for sunshine so I could take Heidi out. She's so full of energy she can scarcely sit still unless she has a good walk. How about you?"

"We're heading home," Anthony said. "Stratton and Peter decided to join us for the walk."

"Well, it was lovely to see you," Lady Emily said, not looking at Callum. "Maybe we can meet tomorrow for tea, Ada. It's been a while since we had the chance for a lengthy chat."

"I'd love that," Ada replied. "But can we make it Friday? I promised my uncle I'd help him at the shop for the next few days."

"Of course," Lady Emily said. "Friday suits me perfectly. I'll invite Harriet too."

"Harriet's also a friend of yours?" Callum asked.

"Yes." Instead of elaborating, Lady Emily dropped into a low crouch and spoke to Peter. "I'm very sorry, but Heidi and I must get going."

Peter looked crestfallen. He sent Callum a hopeful look. "Can't we join them?"

"We mustn't impose," Callum said while Lady Emily shook her head and took a step back, straight into a puddle.

She gasped, and Callum instinctively reached for her. His hand caught her arm, but since that put his body off balance, he took a step forward. At the exact same time as she stepped out of the puddle.

His foot came down over hers and she instantly cried out in pain.

"Sorry. I didn't—"

"Release me," she sputtered while trying to yank her arm free.

He let her go at once. “Please forgive me, Lady Emily. I was only trying to help.”

“I ought to be on my way,” she muttered. “I’ll see you on Friday, Ada. Three o’clock?”

“Looking forward to it,” Ada said and added a smile.

“Come on,” Callum told Peter. “We’ll visit Hatchards and stop by Gunther’s on the way home.”

Peter shrugged one shoulder and gave a despondent, “All right.”

Callum tipped his hat in Lady Emily’s direction. “My apologies once again. Enjoy your walk.”

“What on earth was that?” Anthony asked a few moments later.

“What?” Callum asked.

“You looked like a bloody green boy on wobbly ground. I’ve never seen you so flustered in all my life.” He sent Callum a frown. “I wasn’t even aware men could get flustered until today. And just so you know, you’re still blushing all the way to your ears.”

“I’m not…” Callum groaned with annoyance. “This isn’t a blush. It’s frustration.”

“I think it’s sweet,” Ada told him.

“What?” Callum croaked while Anthony chuckled.

“You’ve clearly taken a fancy to her,” Ada said.

Callum responded with a dry laugh. “I’ve done no such thing. The woman just has the annoying talent of putting herself in the path of my feet or elbows.”

"Considering how suave you usually are in the presence of women," Anthony mused, "I think it might be worth noting when you're not. Especially if there's a pattern."

"Girls can be scary," Peter said, his voice low.

"Lady Emily isn't scary," Callum told him. "She's just incredibly vexing, that's all."

"Is that why you didn't want to walk with her?" Peter asked.

"Yes," Callum told him.

It had nothing to do with the fact that he didn't feel quite himself when she was near.

CHAPTER TWO

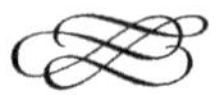

Emily hurried toward the park as fast as she could while Heidi kept pace with her much shorter legs. It was imperative that she add distance between herself and the Duke of Stratton. She should have known that standing near him would be a mistake. Had any other gentleman tried to help her, their foot would never have landed on top of hers

She winced in response to the pain she still felt. Her shoes were made from thin leather and her toes had been crushed beneath his full weight. Checking the street and finding it empty, she crossed toward the park entrance.

Had it not been for him, she *would* have invited Peter to visit so he could spend more time with Heidi. Emily wasn't sure who the boy was or why he was walking with Stratton. As far as she knew, he had no son. Illegitimate or otherwise. And since he had no siblings, the boy could not be his nephew either. Which left few options. In Emily's estimation, Peter was either a distant relation or Stratton's ward.

She slowed her movements while pondering this and gave Heidi a little more leash so it was easier for her to sniff the ground. Peter's expression had been solemn. Too solemn for any child. Of course, he might just be temporarily in Stratton's care while the parents travelled.

Curious, she pondered these various possibilities while continuing through the park. Stratton had never struck her as a family man, so it was interesting to see him assuming a father figure of sorts. In her experience, he'd always been a bit of a rogue – the sort of man who flirted with every woman without ever courting a single one.

Handsome, titled, and seemingly well-poised, he appeared the perfect candidate for England's most eligible bachelor. When seen from afar, that was. Up close, he was an utter disaster. At least from her point of view.

They'd met six years earlier when she'd made her debut. She'd been sixteen and he'd been eighteen, according to Debrett's. It made sense to look him up after returning home from that hellish evening, if for no other reason than to find out who she was dealing with.

Her parents had introduced them. Stratton had

mumbled something about a dance and she had agreed to partner with him. After all, he'd been a duke's heir and she had to admit she'd thought him rather dashing. It was unlikely he'd been similarly impressed by her, for rather than showing excitement, or even a tiny hint of pleasure, he'd looked like he might be sick. A curt nod had followed and then he'd stormed off.

He'd not appeared again until two hours later when it was time for their set. Her interest in partnering with him had been much reduced by then, and it vanished completely when he stepped down on her feet. Not once, twice, or even thrice, but a grand total of thirteen times, leaving her toes so achy and swollen she'd had to sit for the rest of the evening.

One might forgive such an occurrence, and she had. Not everyone was equally gifted when on the dance floor. She herself had struggled with her instructors, so she sympathized. What she did not expect was for it to be the first incident in a series of many.

Keeping to the shorter path that led to the left, she continued walking while Heidi occasionally stopped to sniff. When the dog lingered too long, Emily gently pulled on the leash and the two continued.

Not counting today, she had encountered Stratton on five additional occasions during the last six years. Each had left her increasingly certain that he was best avoided. He must have felt the same way, for they managed to steer completely clear of each other for nearly a year before crossing paths at the Farthington's ball last week.

The fall their encounter had led to was so incredibly typical, she ought to have seen it coming. It was no different from when he'd turned while attempting to move a chair, only to use said chair to knock her into a fountain. There was also the time he had been carrying two large glasses of punch through a crowded room. She'd been coming toward him from the opposite side, their eyes had met, and he'd promptly tripped, spilling the punch all over the front of her white gown.

She also recalled him rushing to help her once when she'd dropped her dance card. Only she'd bent to pick the card up first, bringing her head immediately under his. Not knowing how close he'd come, she'd risen, knocking her head against his so hard her teeth had rattled.

And then there was the time when he'd happened upon her in the park. They'd both been out riding and he'd pulled his horse alongside hers, as one does when one meets an acquaintance and tries to be polite.

Except, he somehow managed to get his stirrup caught in her riding habit. How such a thing was possible she'd never know, but the fact remained that as he rode off, she was pulled from her mount. The only blessing was that it was early morning and that no one besides her groom had borne witness to the embarrassing ordeal.

Finally, there was the Vauxhall Garden incident.

She shuddered.

Her only wish had been to have a nice outing with her parents. But *he'd* been there. Ready as always to ruin everything for her.

She and her parents had gathered to watch the cascade – the waterfall spectacle Vauxhall was so renowned for. The moment she'd seen Stratton approach, she'd moved closer to where her father stood. Unfortunately, Stratton had not seemed the least bit deterred by this. He'd simply waited for the show to end before asking Papa for permission to have a private word with his daughter.

Looking back, Papa had likely believed the conversation would lead to a courtship. He'd allowed it without hesitation, provided Stratton and Emily stayed within view. Stratton had agreed and led Emily farther along the path, to a more secluded spot.

He'd told her how happy he was to see her again and that she looked lovely. All while keeping his gaze on anything other than her. He'd fumbled with something in his pocket and once he retrieved it, he'd launched into a lengthy apology relating to the horse-riding incident. She'd barely understood one word since he kept on losing his focus, interrupting himself and muttering, wrestling with the item he'd found in his pocket.

It turned out to be a box of cheroots. He'd offered her one but she'd declined.

"I accept your apology," she'd told him, watching him strike a flint and light his cheroot. "Accidents happen."

He'd met her gaze and something in his eyes drew her nearer. The smile that followed had been so charmingly bashful she'd rather wished things might have been different between them. But then he'd said, "Unfortunately, you seem to be particularly bad luck for me."

The statement, spoken with an underlying hint of irritation, had set her back on her heels. *She* was bad luck for *him*? If anything, it had to be the other way around. She'd spun away without saying a word, too angry with him to speak. Except he'd leapt around her as if attempting to stop her from leaving, but in doing so, he'd brushed the cheroot he held between his fingers against her swirling skirts.

Emily hadn't even realized what had happened at first. It was Mama who'd called to her about smoking. She'd shaken her head, insisting she wasn't, only to realize her gown had caught fire.

Since then, she'd been very careful to avoid the Duke of Stratton at all costs.

Still, she felt bad for Peter. It had seemed as

though walking Heidi would likely have given him joy. Emily was sorry to have denied that, even if she'd done so for a good reason.

She sighed and started her homeward trek. With the Season well and truly over except for the occasional party, avoiding Stratton for the rest of the year should not be too hard.

Much to her surprise, she realized she was wrong to suppose such a thing when a letter arrived that evening immediately after supper. She was having tea with her mother in the parlor when Larrow, the butler, brought it to her on a silver salver.

"From the Duke of Stratton, my lady."

Emily stared at the missive, half afraid to touch it in case the duke had somehow managed to poison it. She'd not put it past him.

"Go on," said Mama. "Take it."

Emily took a deep breath and picked up the letter. It had been neatly folded and sealed with a shiny blob of crimson wax bearing the Stratton insignia. A bold script on the front bore her name.

Much to Emily's astonishment, her heart began beating slightly faster. She fiddled with the paper while taking deep breaths in an effort to steady her pulse.

"Aren't you going to read it?" Mama asked while refilling their teacups.

Emily nodded. The room felt uncomfortably hot all of a sudden. "Of course."

She tore the seal as carefully as she could so she might preserve it, and unfolded the paper.

Dear Lady Emily,

I hope this letter finds you well. Hopefully, your toes have recovered from the brutality they were subjected to this afternoon, although to be fair, I wouldn't have stepped on them, had you been more aware of your surroundings. But since I did do the stepping, I'd like to extend an apology, though this is not my only reason for writing.

While I realize our history has not been the best, I am hoping you will set it aside long enough to consider my humble request. What I ask, is for Peter to be allowed to spend additional time with Heidi. However inconvenient this may be for either of us, that dog is the first thing to capture his interest since his parents died. I cannot in good conscience ignore that and pray you won't either.

In anticipation of your response,

Callum Davis, Duke of Stratton.

Emily re-read the letter three times while trying to figure out what to make of it. She wasn't sure whether she ought to feel vexed, touched, or slightly afraid. His suggestion that she was equally to blame for him stepping upon her toes was beyond the pale. But then he'd mentioned Peter's response to Heidi and Emily's heart had melted. She wanted to accommodate Stratton's request, but she also feared doing so might cause her additional harm.

"Well?" Mama asked. "What does he say?"

"Nothing much," Emily lied. She refolded the letter and tucked it inside her skirt pocket. "He merely wished to apologize for setting my gown on fire that one time."

She would not mention today's interaction with him since she had no wish to answer whatever questions it might lead to. As far as her parents knew, there had only been the one mishap concerning her gown, which was also the worst one by far. But they'd been completely unaware of the rest. Each time an incident had occurred, she'd made an excuse, leaving Stratton's name out of it. No one saw what had happened and she'd deliberately chosen to save him from the humiliation.

Frowning, she now wondered at that decision.

"But that was ages ago," Mama said. "As I recall, he begged our forgiveness when it happened."

"Yes." It was the only time he'd managed to say he was sorry, and only then because her parents were present. Had they not been, she would have cut him off as she usually did and asked him to leave her alone. She sighed. Maybe she wasn't as kind as she thought herself to be.

She glanced at Mama. "Do you mind if I retire? I'm feeling a little tired."

"By all means. Get some rest, Emily. You mustn't

linger on my account."

"Thank you." Emily went and pressed a kiss to her mother's cheek. "I'll see you tomorrow. Goodnight."

When she arrived in her bedchamber, Emily rang for her lady's maid, Georgina, to help her change into a nightgown and comb out her hair. Once this had been done and Georgina had left, Emily put on her dressing gown, then took a seat at her desk.

The letter from Stratton lay before her, demanding a response.

She took a deep breath and collected a crisp piece of foolscap. After dipping her quill in her inkwell, she took a moment to gather her thoughts before writing,

Dear Duke of Stratton,

I thank you for your letter, which was well received. While I will admit stepping into that puddle was no one's fault but my own, my toes would not have been squished had you remained where you were. I did not require your aid but appreciate your apology. As for your request, I would like to do what I can to make Peter happy, though I do have a small request in return – that you and I maintain a safe distance apart at all times. If this suits, please bring Peter to Hyde Park tomorrow so he and Heidi can play. I'll be at the entrance, ten o'clock sharp.

Lady Emily Brooke

CHAPTER THREE

Callum stared at Lady Emily's missive. She'd taken responsibility for stepping into the puddle, though not without insulting him in the process. He wasn't sure what to think about that, but one thing was certain – he'd have liked to tell her the day and hour did not suit. Hell, he'd have liked to inform her that he no longer wished to meet.

Were it not for Peter.

Callum expelled a weary breath, set the missive aside, and went back to eating his breakfast. He would put his constant conflict with Lady Emily behind him for the sake of his ward.

A decision that saw him escorting a very excited Peter toward Hyde Park the following morning. Thankfully, Lady Emily had asked that she and Callum keep some distance from each other. This suited Callum fine. He'd not have to speak with her and would hopefully avoid getting blamed for additional mishaps.

What he didn't expect, was the hollowness that settled behind his breastbone a half hour later, even as he watched Peter throw a stick for Heidi to chase. The boy cheered and clapped his hands, grinning when Heidi returned the stick to him so he could throw it again. It was marvelous. Callum was thrilled to have found a way to bring him some joy. And yet, there was an underlying sense of wrongness with the world that Callum couldn't quite place.

He glanced across at Lady Emily, who sat on a bench roughly ten yards away while he leaned against a tree. Of course he'd greeted her and the maid she'd brought with her when he and Peter arrived. Anything less would have been unbelievably rude. But it hadn't amounted to more than a nod and a tip of his hat since he'd every intention of honoring her request. As such, he'd kept his distance when Peter went to collect the leash Lady Emily held toward him.

She'd dipped her chin in acknowledgement of Callum's greeting, after which she and Peter had entered the park while Callum and the maid followed behind. The entire situation had felt rather awkward. Something he'd like to avoid if they met again, as Peter had asked that they do as soon as they'd started their homeward trek.

Callum scratched the nape of his neck. Surely

there had to be some way for him and Lady Emily to overcome their differences. Knitting his brow, he opened his desk drawer and retrieved the missive she'd sent in response to his own. He unfolded it and read it once more, acknowledging this time that her point was no less valid than the one he'd attempted to make in his missive to her.

They were both responsible for their unfortunate interactions with each other over the years, and in order for them to get past the wariness this had instilled in each of them, they'd have to talk.

With this in mind, Callum placed another piece of foolscap on his desk, dipped his quill in the inkwell, and proceeded to write.

Emily considered the most recent missive Stratton had sent her with some apprehension. He wanted to meet with her for a private talk, which obviously meant coming into close vicinity of each other. She flattened her mouth while pondering this. Their last outing had gone well enough. Nothing untoward had happened. She'd been fine.

Then again, Stratton had remained at a safe distance throughout the park visit.

Emily tapped the side of her mouth with a finger. She wondered what he wished to discuss. Clearly, something he'd rather say in person than put into writing. Perhaps a matter regarding Peter? Or something else?

She'd no idea. But what she *did* know was that if she agreed to this rendezvous, there was a good chance she'd end up in yet another sprawl. Or worse.

Then again, she was curious. And besides, it would be unkind of her to deny him when he had insisted it would mean a great deal to him if she would accommodate this wish.

Very well then. But it would be on her terms.

This request saw her seated at one end of a park bench the following afternoon while Stratton sat at the other. Close enough to chat but with enough separation between them to hopefully prevent a calamity. Emily's maid, Georgina, remained nearby for propriety's sake, allowing Emily to speak with the duke without being overhead, though for the moment, neither uttered a word.

After greeting each other politely and taking their seats, silence followed. Emily smoothed her skirt over her knees and waited. The leaves from a nearby tree rustled in the breeze. She watched a few people stroll by some distance away – a group of ladies walking their dogs and a husband and wife with their three children.

"You may not believe me when I tell you this," Stratton finally said. Though his voice was soft, he applied a serious tone that drew her complete attention. "But it has never been my intention to cause you harm. Every accident you've been subjected to while in my company, has been precisely that. An accident."

"As much as I'd like to take your word for that, an accident is something that happens once. Possibly twice. Not every time two people meet." She shook her head while thinking back. "And besides, you always seemed annoyed with me for some reason. It's only natural for me to wonder if all the incidents our chance meetings led to were calculated in nature."

"I can assure you they were not. And if I ever spoke to you curtly, it was only because I allowed *your* reaction to rile me."

"I beg your pardon?"

"This was wrong," he hastened to add while angling himself toward her. "You were right to be vexed when our every encounter led to disaster, but your unwillingness to accept my apologies rankled. Especially since I am not the only one at fault. After all, you were there too, reacting to my every move."

"Go on," she urged, shivering slightly when a cool breeze brushed the nape of her neck. She didn't like what he implied, but she wasn't too proud to concede that one could easily overlook one's own faults. So if she'd played a part in their unharmonious relationship, she needed to know. Especially if she'd unwittingly wronged him.

"When you and I danced at your debut, you

turned the wrong way more than once, causing several of my missteps."

"I suppose that's true," she said, recalling how nervous she'd been that evening. Could it be that he'd felt the same way?

"When I knocked you into the fountain, it was because you happened to move to the right at the same exact moment I turned to the left."

"I never realized..."

"When we met that one time during our morning rides, your skirt would not have been caught in my stirrup had you remained where you were. But you were impatient to be on your way and started forward too soon while we were too close."

She swallowed and forced herself to meet his gaze. Was it possible Stratton's point was valid? Could it be he was not the only one to blame for the various mishaps she had endured while in his company? "What about Vauxhall?"

"Vauxhall, I'll grant you, was entirely my fault. Since I'm at least partially to blame for the rest, however, and you never allowed me the chance to apologize, I'd like to do so now. Properly. Hence my reason for asking you here." He paused for a second and when he spoke next, his voice was filled with endless sincerity. "Please forgive me for any bodily harm and embarrassment I may have caused you since our introduction."

Taken aback by his sudden show of integrity,

Emily gazed at him for a moment until the expectant look in his eyes made her blink.

"Of course." She appreciated the apology and could not avoid the niggling guilt taking hold of her conscience. Even if she had been increasingly frustrated by him and every incident his presence led to, she'd been wrong to deny him the chance to apologize. It had been unkind, she reflected.

"If you'd like to push me into a pond in return, you need only name the time and place."

She grinned in response to his jovial tone and instantly felt the air between them grow lighter. "That won't be necessary. And besides, given our history, I'd probably fall in with you."

He laughed and agreed this might be a likely outcome, which made her smile. A bit of companionable silence followed before she said, "I need to ask your forgiveness too. It appears I've been unfair toward you and for that I am deeply sorry. Denying you the chance to apologize was wrong."

"I could have written to you sooner."

Deciding there was no point in arguing this, Emily merely dipped her head. When Stratton said nothing further, she eventually stood. "I ought to get home, but I'm glad we had this discussion."

When he stood too and stepped toward her as though intending to reach for her hand, she retreated, placing herself beyond his reach. He gave her a sheepish grin. "Too soon?"

"Just a little."

"I'll wish you a pleasant day then, my lady."

She echoed the sentiment and departed, accompanied by Georgina.

It pleased her to know she'd made the correct decision in meeting with Stratton. Their conversation had been productive, allowing them to make amends and let bygones be bygones.

Even so, an odd sensation shadowed her all the way home. It almost felt like regret. For six years, she and Stratton had been at odds. Their cat and mouse game had defined every social event she'd ever attended. He'd bothered her to no end. She'd done what she could to avoid him.

There was something strange about that coming to an end. It was almost like the world had fallen off its axis.

Disturbed by this notion, she decided to try and forget the duke altogether by getting on with her day. They'd made no additional plans to meet, which suited her perfectly. Why wouldn't it? To suppose she was disappointed that he'd not suggested another outing with Heidi and Peter would be absurd.

Besides, with two books left to finish before she could start on the one Ada had brought her, she didn't have time for dukish pursuits. Plus, Ada, and possibly Harriet, would be coming for tea tomorrow afternoon. It would be nice to get some reading done before then.

"Is everything all right?" Harriet asked her the following day.

She and Ada had arrived roughly twenty minutes ago. Tea had been served along with a tasty lemon cake topped with meringue, and a conversation pertaining to suggestions for the book club's next monthly read had begun.

"Hmm?" Emily stared at her friend and was shocked when she couldn't recall the last thing that had been said. All she remembered was Ada mentioning *The Vicar of Wakefield,* and that was a while ago.

"You seem distracted." Harriet peered at her with concern. "Is something troubling you?"

"No." Emily shook her head, reached for her tea, and smiled reassuringly at her friends. She would not let them know that she'd been distracted by a particular duke. "I was merely trying to work out whether or not I should put *The Touchstone* and *Melincourt* on hold so I'll be ready with my review of *Seductive Scandal* for release day."

"You've always had a first come first served policy," Ada said. "Please don't give me special treatment."

Emily nodded. There was no need to of course. She was a fast reader and knew she'd have all three books read within a couple of weeks. But it had given her the excuse she'd required.

"Right." Emily sipped her tea. "I think Fanny Burney's *The Wanderer* is an excellent choice for the book club's next novel. Plenty of—"

The door opened after a quick knock and Larrow entered, bringing with him a silver salver. Emily gripped her armrest to keep herself seated. It wouldn't do to leap from her chair and snatch up the letter Larrow had brought, although she could barely contain her excitement. Was it from Stratton and if so, what did it say?

Her heart raced while a fluttery sort of feeling began taking root in her stomach.

Not wishing for her friends to pry, however, she used whatever superhuman strength she was capable of to maintain her composure. It wasn't easy to do when she saw the missive was indeed from the duke. Taking it from the salver without looking like she was desperate to know what it said, tested the full extent of her ability to remain calm.

"Thank you, Larrow." The butler gave a curt nod and departed, leaving Emily with the guilt of wishing her friends would soon leave. All she wanted right now was to run upstairs, lock her bedchamber door, and learn what Stratton had written.

It took another two hours before the chance to do so arose. But as soon as she'd wished her friends a wonderful rest of the day and seen them off, Mama came to ask for her help in choosing the fabric for a new gown she intended to order. This took an additional ten minutes, after which Emily finally managed to find the privacy she desired.

She retrieved the letter from her skirt pocket and stared at her name as though trying to find some hidden meaning within the elegant slant of each letter.

Foolish.

You don't even like him so why all the fuss?

Annoyed with herself, she scooted into the window seat overlooking the garden, tore the seal, and proceeded to read.

My dear Lady Emily,

Our most recent conversation has made me reflect on a great many things, most notably your refusal to seek the justice you deserve. A lesser person would have leapt at the chance to push me into a pond. By denying yourself, you not only saved me from the humiliation you yourself were subjected to at my hands, but you also showed great consideration toward my clothing, which would without doubt have been ruined.

I hope therefore to extend my thanks. Preferably in person. In my experience, flowers are best delivered that way.

Will you let me stop by?

Callum Davis, Duke of Stratton.

. . .

Emily took a sharp breath. She'd grinned in response to his comment regarding his clothing, but then he'd mentioned flowers and to be honest, it felt like she might be blushing. Was that even possible, and if so, how? Stratton had never been charming while in her presence. He'd never attempted to be, as far as she knew. Yet here he was now, offering explanations and apologies, then asking if he might call upon her with flowers.

Her heart fluttered while instinct warned her not to get carried away. This was Stratton. The bane of her existence for six long years.

And yet, she was starting to think she'd misjudged him right from the start. For although she'd always found him too curt, aloof, or seemingly uncaring whenever she'd spoken to him, he showed a great deal of fondness and concern for Peter. She'd seen him console the boy, doing what few fathers would do in public. He'd pulled the boy close and hugged him, which appeared to mean that the man was much more than what he pretended to be.

Either that, or she'd never been given the chance to properly get to know him. Truth was, she'd not really wanted to after the first time they'd danced.

But now?

She sat back. Even if his apology and the flowers he wished to bring were offered solely because of Peter, it occurred to Emily that the sort of man who would go to such lengths on account of a child was rare. He was worth knowing and deserved her full attention.

With this in mind, she retrieved a fresh piece of foolscap and wrote her response.

Dear Duke of Stratton,

You are welcome to stop by whenever you wish. Flowers are always welcome, though I recommend something other than roses since they carry thorns.

Looking forward to seeing you soon.

Lady Emily Brooke.

CHAPTER FOUR

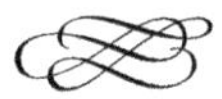

Callum grinned in response to the latest letter he'd just received from Lady Emily. He hadn't realized she possessed such sharp wit. How would he when they'd never spoken at great length? She'd responded to him in kind though, matching him every step of the way. It occurred to him he'd looked forward to her response. More than he cared to admit.

Ah, who was he trying to fool?

She'd always affected him. From the very first moment he saw her, dressed in white beaded lace and with her hair styled in a way that softened her features. No other lady had equaled her beauty that evening. As a result, he'd made an absolute arse of himself ever since.

It was time to change that. Time for him to pull himself together and stop getting flustered around her. He had to do it for Peter, and in his estimation, his efforts so far were proving effective. Their conversation in the park the previous day had gone better than he'd expected. She'd not only listened, she'd also made an apology of her own.

It was a start, though it would have been better if he'd thought to make future plans for them to meet. Somehow, doing so had escaped him completely until he'd returned home and Peter had asked about seeing Heidi again. Honestly, he could have smacked himself, for the truth was he'd been so relieved over saying what needed saying without doing something stupid to boot, everything else had slipped his mind.

Naturally, he'd promised Peter he'd ask about an additional outing. But when he'd sat down to write the request, he'd worried it might sound as though he'd apologized to Lady Emily solely for the sake of gaining access to her dog. Which wouldn't do at all since it risked undoing the effort he'd made thus far.

He, therefore, decided to tread with more care. Which led to the idea of bringing her flowers.

What he hadn't expected was the pure delight this exchange with her had led to. He'd been amused. Which was wholly unexpected because of how rude he'd believed her to be.

But was she really? The truth was he'd never gotten to know her. The chance to do so had never been there. However, based upon her correspondence, he was starting to think he might have been missing out.

With this in mind, he set off for her house that same afternoon. She had said he'd be welcome whenever he wished, and frankly, he'd rather not wait.

Anticipation raced through his veins. When he stopped by the hothouse on the way and the woman behind the counter suggested roses, he dismissed the idea. Instead, he selected flowers he didn't know the names of, but they were pretty and brightly colored with accents of green. A lovely and rather unique bouquet, he decided.

Perfectly suited for Lady Emily.

He arrived at her home a good ten minutes later. The butler took his hat and gloves, then led him directly to the parlor where Callum's presence was promptly announced.

Glimpsing Lady Emily, he took a deep breath and attempted to tamp down the old familiar queasiness gripping his stomach. It never happened in anyone else's presence.

It took some effort for him to ignore the frantic beat of his pulse as he walked through the door, gripping the bouquet as though it would offer support. For some absurd reason, calling on Lady Emily at her home made him far more nervous than meeting her in the park. There was a certain formality to coming here with a bouquet of flowers.

Good heavens.

He hoped she wouldn't think he'd embarked on a courtship.

Casting that possibility aside for the sake of pure self-preservation, he swept the room with his gaze. It was a lovely space, furnished mostly in creamy tones that were accented by hints of sky blue.

He sucked in a breath the moment he found her. Heat washed the back of his neck and his palms grew clammy. Unsure of himself, he was suddenly terrified he might cause some other mishap. Like tripping over the carpet and sending the flowers flying, or worse, landing upon the low table before her and knocking the teapot into her lap.

She stood, with the same sort of hesitance he'd decided he'd best apply. "Welcome, Your Grace. Please have a seat."

Callum took quick stock of any potential obstacles in his path. Finding none, he approached the armchair she'd gestured toward. The maid who'd joined Lady Emily on her previous outings to the park sat a few yards away, her attention on some piece of mending she busied herself with while serving as chaperone.

"Thank you for seeing me." Callum cleared his throat and pushed the flowers toward her. "These are for you."

She smiled with what appeared to be genuine warmth in her eyes. The sight was so dazzling he forgot himself for a second and didn't realize she was attempting to take the bouquet while he continued to grip it.

"Sorry," he muttered, letting the flowers go. He cleared his throat again and started to sit, only to realize that she still stood. He quickly straightened himself once more while silently cursing himself for his foolish behavior.

Get a hold of yourself, man. She must think you're stupid.

"They're lovely," she said right before she pressed her nose to the flowers and took a deep breath. "I think this may be my favorite bouquet to date."

Heat rushed to Callum's cheeks. He averted his gaze and scrubbed a hand across his jaw to hide the embarrassing effect of her words. "I'm glad you approve."

She gave him a funny look before turning toward the maid. "Georgina, can you please find a vase for these?"

"Of course, my lady."

"And please bring a fresh pot of tea with an extra cup when you return. Some of Cook's freshly baked rhubarb tarts would be lovely as well."

The maid departed, leaving Callum alone with Lady Emily though the door to the parlor remained wide open. No chance of getting up to mischief here. Not that he would consider it. Although thinking of *not* considering it made him ponder exactly that. His gaze shifted to Lady Emily. To her mouth in particular, and, for a second, he allowed himself to wonder what it might be like to kiss her.

Delicious.

"Your Grace?"

"Yes?"

"I was suggesting we sit." She studied him a moment. "Unless you merely intended to drop off the flowers and leave."

He laughed, the sound a touch too nervous for his liking. "No. I'd like to stay for a bit if you've no other plans."

"None besides reading." She lowered herself to the sofa and he took the armchair adjacent to it.

"Do you read a great deal then?"

"As often as I can. It's my greatest passion."

"Really?" He was slightly surprised. The Lady Emily he'd seen over the years hadn't struck him as a bluestocking. "What's your favorite book?"

"An impossible question for me to answer."

He raised an eyebrow. "Which have you reread the greatest number of times?"

She averted her gaze and fiddled a bit with her skirts before saying, "You'll think it silly, I'm sure, but it's actually *Celestina*."

"Why would I think that silly?" He smiled and relaxed in her presence for the first time. "I must have read that book a dozen times."

"Truly?" She stared at him with wide-eyed amazement. "You're not jesting?"

He leaned forward slightly and affected his most serious tone. "I would never jest about such an uplifting novel."

She grinned, and in that moment, everything changed. Callum couldn't explain it, but he felt like a bit of a fool. Somehow, he'd allowed his first encounter with her to guide every subsequent interaction. He'd managed to tie himself into knots over thinking of how to approach her and what he should say once he did. As a result, he'd always moved too quickly while in her presence, and this had made him clumsy.

Now, he wondered *why* she'd made him so nervous. She was, as it turned out, quite normal.

"What's your favorite part of the story?"

Callum considered her question with care before giving his answer. "I believe it must be the duel."

"I love that too, though I think my favorite part is when Willoughby discovers the truth about Celestina's birth and realizes they are free to marry."

"You're absolutely right. How could I have forgotten?"

She beamed at him without answering that. "What's your favorite pastime activity?"

"One would think it's pestering you." He was glad when she laughed in response to the joke. "In truth, it's actually writing."

"Oh?" She looked visibly intrigued and appeared as though she might say more on the subject, but then the maid returned and distracted her. A fresh pot of tea was placed on the table along with a teacup intended for Callum. A plate filled with four rhubarb tarts was set beside it. Lady Emily thanked the maid, and then, much to Callum's surprise, she said, "I know you have duties to attend to, Georgina, so feel free to leave us."

The maid bobbed a curtsey and departed. The door, Callum noted, remained wide open. Still, he could not help but ask, "You're not worried you might need a witness in case I trip over my feet while attempting to stand?"

"I sent her away so there *won't* be anyone here to see if something like that occurs," she told him wryly. "Thought I'd protect your pride."

He met her gaze with a laugh. The sparkle of pure amusement he found there went straight to his heart. Had he known she'd been this delightful he'd not have wasted six years steering clear of her or blaming her for turning him into an awkward idiot.

"I'm truly sorry for all of my blunders." He'd told her so already, but it was the sort of thing that warranted repeating. "My intention was never to cause you harm or embarrassment. It was purely accidental."

"So you've said, and I believe you." She poured the tea. "Perhaps we can speak of your writing instead? I'm curious to know if you've ever been published."

"I have not." Thankfully this was the truth. The book he'd helped his friends write had been printed, but one couldn't truly say it was published until it was made available in a shop. He picked up his cup. "It's just a hobby, you see – a way for me to escape the world in a more responsible way than I used to."

He didn't miss the look of sympathy in her eyes, but rather than question what he might need to escape from, she asked, "What's your preference? Poetry or novels?"

"Short stories," he said. Having set his cup aside, he indicated the tarts. "May I?"

"By all means. Please help yourself." She pushed the plate toward him and waited for him to select a tart before selecting her own. "And what sort of style would you say you favor?"

"It's a bit of a mixed bag, to be honest. I suppose my mood sets the tone." He bit into the flaky tart crust, catching Lady Emily's gaze as she did the same. A laugh rolled through him, and her eyes, he noted, danced with humor. Not that there was any particular reason for it besides simply feeling at ease.

"Would you ever allow me to read some of it?" she asked once she'd finished eating.

Callum swallowed the last bite he'd taken and opened his mouth, prepared to answer, when the sight of her licking her fingers rendered him mute.

She seemed not to care that he saw, and this had a couple of very opposing effects.

On the one hand, he liked that she was comfortable enough in his presence to do the most practical thing instead of what was considered most proper. On the other, however, *she was sitting right there, licking her fingers!*

While holding his gaze, no less. And smiling.

He would have shredded his napkin, had it been made of paper. The sight was so bloody provocative, his blood started to sizzle. Heaven have mercy, the woman was born to be a seductress.

"Well?" she asked.

Well, what?

He tried to marshal his thoughts. What had she been saying? Oh right. Would he let her read his writing.

"I'm not sure that would be wise."

"Whyever not?"

"Because you love reading." He picked up his teacup and set it to his lips. "I'd hate to change that."

Her answering laugh was instant. "Not a chance, but I shan't press. If you ever do feel inclined to request an honest opinion of your work, I'm happy to oblige."

"Thank you, I'll keep that in mind." It would never happen. He'd rather die than let anyone read his stories while knowing he was the one who'd penned them.

A comfortable silence followed before she spoke next. "Your first letter to me was an unexpected surprise. You've never attempted to contact me before."

"You're right." His gaze went to Heidi, who was curled into a tiny ball on the carpet. "I did it for Peter."

"Of course you did."

His gaze shot toward her just in time to catch the pained look on her face. He could have kicked himself in the shin just then. Putting doubt in her mind was the last thing he wanted. "Please don't misunderstand me. I'm glad you and I are talking. It's taken too long to get to this point, but I didn't simply decide to seek you out for you alone."

Oh, for the love of God, stop putting your foot in your mouth.

She'd narrowed her gaze and who could blame her?

He prepared to explain, but before he could find the right words she asked, "Was the apology genuine?"

"Of course it was."

"I want to believe you, but I'm not sure I do."

"I haven't lied to you, Emily." He froze at the realization that he'd foregone the use of the honorific. "Sorry. Slip of the tongue, my lady. I, um…"

Lady Emily stared at him as though trying to work out what might be wrong with his brain.

Breaking eye contact, she tilted her head. A crease appeared on her brow. "Whether or not your apology was sincere, I cannot fault you for trying to make a child happy. Who is he to you?"

Callum sighed. "He's my cousin's son. He and his wife perished a few months ago in a fire. The will left Peter in my care."

"Oh dear." Lady Emily's hand came to rest over his for a second before she snatched it away as if burned. "I'm so incredibly sorry." Her eyes glistened. "How absolutely awful. That poor boy."

Callum flexed his fingers. He could still feel the spark from her touch gently burning beneath his skin.

"My father's death destroyed me three years ago, and I was already a man. I can't imagine what it must be like for Peter. We were practically strangers, he and I, until I was asked to come and collect him. He's my responsibility now, but I don't know how to help. Nothing seems to offer him comfort, or at least it didn't until we met you last week while you were out walking.

"His response to Heidi gave me hope. That's why I'm here. The main reason, at least. Playing with her in the park the other day made an impact on him. He's started talking more, but much of what he says pertains to future interactions with Heidi."

"And you worried there wouldn't be any since we made no additional plans?"

"You didn't invite us to join you again so I thought you might have considered the outing a one-time occurrence. That's why I'm here. Because Peter needs this."

"You could have told me all of this yesterday when we met." She tilted her head as if in thought. "Why didn't you?"

"Honestly, I forgot." He felt monumentally stupid.

She pressed her lips together as though to stifle a laugh. "That's actually a perfectly sound excuse."

"Later," he admitted, "when I finally thought to send another request, I feared you might suspect me of taking advantage. Coming here in person, allowing you to get to know me a little bit better, seemed like a better course of action. One more likely to meet with success."

"We're speaking of helping a child." Her voice was slightly sad, her eyes more so as they stared back at his. "Did you really think I'd refuse?"

"I don't know. Perhaps not. I'm honestly not sure."

She was quiet for a long moment, during which Callum prayed he'd not said the wrong thing. He watched as she drank some more tea, then as she worried her lower lip, all while holding his breath.

Eventually, she said, "I realize Peter might prefer playing with Heidi, but she also needs to go for walks. I take her every morning after breaking my fast. You're welcome to join me if you like."

"Peter and I would love that," Callum said as he expelled his breath.

"Let's meet at the Hyde Park entrance tomorrow morning then. Will ten o'clock suit?"

"Perfectly so. Thank you."

"Hopefully, with a bit of common sense and caution, you and I can prevent another accident from occurring."

"I shall certainly do my best to keep you out of harm's way," he promised.

"Thank you, Your Grace."

He glanced at the two remaining rhubarb tarts. They were awfully good, but since he sensed their conversation was at an end, he abandoned the idea of having another and stood. "Until tomorrow, my lady."

She bid him farewell and he left with a smile. He was not only pleased with the progress he'd made for Peter's sake, but for his own as well. Lady Emily, as it turned out, was not only pretty. She was also a lovely person whose company he'd enjoyed a lot more than he had expected. His heart thumped with the excitement of seeing her again soon.

He only hoped he wouldn't ruin what had the potential of turning into a marvelous friendship.

CHAPTER FIVE

Even though she'd told herself repeatedly not to get excited over the idea of seeing Stratton again, Emily's heart still skipped a beat when she saw him the following morning. Handsomely dressed in a dark-blue jacket, fawn-colored breeches, and black boots, he cast an imposing figure as she made her approach. They would not be alone of course. Peter was with him and she'd brought Georgina as well, but they would still talk and interact.

Their meeting yesterday had been full of surprises. She'd not expected to enjoy Stratton's company quite as much as she had. He'd proven himself a fun and interesting conversationalist. There was no denying it had stung when she'd realized he'd not asked to see her for her sake alone.

But she'd forgiven the slight in a heartbeat. How

could she not when the man was attempting to make his ward happy? Him reaching out to her, a woman he'd feared might reject the olive branch he tried to offer, proved he was kind, selfless, and brave.

Considerate too, she reflected, recalling the bouquet he'd brought her. He'd not only done as she'd asked and forgone the traditional bouquet of roses, he'd also pleased her with the vibrant and cheerful collection of flowers he'd offered in its place.

All in all, sitting down with him over tea had been a pleasant affair. Nothing disastrous had happened. He'd seemed a bit tense at first but then he'd relaxed and the afternoon together had progressed without any issue.

This gave her hope. It also made her wonder about things she probably ought not be wondering about. Like why she'd felt a spark of awareness when she touched his hand, or if he'd felt it too. Such questions could only lead to trouble, so she did her best to push them aside and to focus on her purpose. Today was about Peter.

"Good morning," she said once she reached the pair. "I hope you're ready for a long walk. Heidi enjoys her exercise."

Peter had already dropped to a crouch so he could pet Heidi. He grinned when she licked at his chin with her tongue.

"Thank you." Stratton mouthed the words when

Emily's gaze caught his. The smile that followed was filled with so much gratitude, her heart immediately tripled in size.

She gave a quick nod for the sake of maintaining her composure. Apparently, the duke could be rather charming when he wasn't tripping her up. "I thought you might like to hold the leash, Peter."

The boy instantly stood, his eyes bright with near disbelief. "May I?"

"Of course." Emily handed the leash to Peter and showed him how to hold it. "Don't lengthen it too much or you run the risk of its getting tangled."

They entered the park and proceeded along the main path. Peter walked slightly ahead of Emily and Stratton, who strolled side by side while Georgina followed behind at a distance.

"Thank you again for doing this," Stratton said after a while. He kept his voice low, so Peter wouldn't hear, but added a sense of intimacy to his tone. The effect was rather potent. It warmed her cheeks and made her feel slightly breathless.

Pretending to admire the landscape so he wouldn't notice, she said, "I'm happy to help."

He said nothing else for a while afterward and that, she decided, wasn't bad either. She didn't feel a pressing need to fill the silence as she sometimes did with other people. With Stratton, she realized she found it rather pleasant, as though them simply being there together, was enough.

It was most peculiar and very unexpected.

"Shall we purchase some treats?" Stratton asked when a vendor came into view.

Peter glanced back at him with a happy nod. "Yes, please."

Emily looked at Stratton. His face was more severe in profile, but the smile he sent Peter softened the edges. Disturbed that she'd even notice such a thing, she clasped her hands behind her back and agreed that a treat would be lovely.

"Here you are," said Stratton once the vendor had finished preparing four portions of sweetmeats. They'd been wrapped in brown paper cones so they could be easily carried.

Stratton handed the first one to Emily, the second to Georgina, whom he'd been thoughtful enough to consider, and the third one to Peter.

"That'll be sixpence," said the vendor.

Emily pulled on the strings of her reticule.

Stratton frowned at her. "What are you doing?"

"Searching for the right coins."

"Absolutely not." He'd placed his hand over hers to stop her movements. Their eyes met and her stomach instantly tightened while everything else slid into the background. His voice when next he spoke was firm. "I'll pay."

"But—"

"I insist." He removed his hand from hers and

collected some coins from his pocket, then counted them out quickly and gave them to the vendor.

"Thank you, Your Grace," said Georgina. She peered at her cone with utter delight.

Emily stared at Stratton in wonder, then remembered to thank him as well. His touch had left her a bit lightheaded. Or maybe she'd simply not eaten enough for breakfast?

Puzzled, she followed Peter who'd just resumed walking, and selected a green piece of sweetmeat from her cone. She popped it into her mouth and savored the tangy flavor of lime dipped in sugar. They'd been lucky today with the weather, which could be so unpredictable this time of year. Instead of rain, the sun shone from a cloudless sky and the air was warm enough for her to be comfortable without having to wear a spencer, though she had brought a shawl.

The path curved up ahead as they approached the lake. A dog barked in the distance and someone started shouting. Emily turned and almost dropped her sweetmeats. The dog was massive and it was charging directly toward them with a young man in pursuit. Both barely managed to avoid a lady riding a horse. The horse reared, the lady screamed, and now she too was coming their way at a mad gallop.

Emily spun toward Peter who'd not yet realized he was about to get trampled. So was Heidi. The other dog was headed straight for her while the runaway horse bore down on Peter. Emily leapt forward while shouting his name. He turned and froze, so she did the only thing she could think of. Propelled by instinct, she tossed her sweetmeats aside and shoved Peter forward, placing herself in the horse's path instead.

She prepared to get out of the way, but the massive dog arrived before she was able and blocked her escape. The horse's breath landed upon her face and Emily said a quick prayer. Someone grabbed her upper arm and she flew backward, straight into a solid surface.

"I've got you," a low voice murmured against her cheek.

Emily blinked and she realized she was wrapped in a strong embrace. Stratton was holding her from behind, one arm wound tightly around her waist, the other still gripping her arm. His chest rose and fell with rough movements against her back. For a second his hold tightened, as though he were hugging her to him, before he relaxed.

He slowly released her, and as he turned her to face him, she realized his hands were shaking. The depth of concern in his eyes nearly stole her breath.

"Are you all right?" Clutching her shoulders he swept his gaze over her body as though seeking proof that she was unharmed.

She nodded. "Yes. I am well. But what about Peter and Heidi?"

Stratton straightened and released her completely. "Georgina has them. Peter will be fine, thanks to you, and I believe Heidi avoided harm too. From what I've managed to gather these past few seconds, the larger dog simply wanted to come and greet her."

"You ought to keep that dog on a leash," said the lady riding the horse. Having finally managed to reign in her mount and circle back to join the group, she glared in anger at the young man.

"I'm terribly sorry," the young man replied. He did look remorseful. "Hercules has a leash. See? He just managed to pull it out of my grasp. It was an accident."

"One that could have ended in tragedy," Stratton informed him, his voice suddenly hard and unyielding. "In the future, I'd ask you to make sure a stronger man walks your dog."

"Of course."

Stratton jerked his head to one side and the young man hurried away, pulling Hercules after him. The lady on the horse gave Stratton a curt nod before moving away at a trot. With tension still rippling off him, Stratton crossed to where Georgina waited together with Peter and Heidi. Oblivious to the danger that had occurred a few moments ago, the dog sat on the ground wagging her tail as if all of this had been wonderfully entertaining.

Emily went to her while Stratton checked on Peter.

"Are you unharmed?" Emily heard him ask of the boy.

She saw Peter nod out of the corner of her eye while she stroked Heidi's back and proceeded to scratch her behind one ear.

"Lady Emily saved me," Peter added, his voice filled with so much awe that it was impossible for Emily to keep from smiling. She was pleased to know the boy thought well of her.

"I saw," Stratton said. "It was incredibly brave of her."

Her smile wobbled in response to the strong emotion that suddenly gripped her. The way he said it, as though he'd never been more impressed by anyone in his life, completely undid her. After all the clashes they'd had, having his praise was immensely rewarding.

She gave Heidi's head a final pat before rising.

"You got me out of harm's way for once," she told Stratton as soon as he'd straightened to stand beside her. "I'm grateful."

He caught her gaze and the warmth she saw there heated her insides. "As am I."

"Can we buy some more sweetmeats?' asked Peter. "Most of mine fell to the ground."

Emily chuckled while glancing about. The ground was littered with colorful bits of confection.

She caught Stratton's gaze and shrugged one shoulder. "What do you think?"

"I say we need a refill." He grinned and so did she. They returned to the vendor together.

"Will you let me pay this time?"

"Absolutely not." When she arched her brow and prepared to protest, he told her softly, "Perhaps when we have our next outing?"

He wanted to see her again? The knowledge delighted her beyond measure. So much, in fact, she immediately grinned.

How curious it was that she should be so thrilled to spend additional time with a man she'd dreaded running into a few days before. Getting to know him was proving to be not only enlightening but also highly enjoyable. Now that he'd saved her, she even felt safe around him, which was something she would have believed impossible until now.

"Would you like to rest for a while?" Stratton asked when they were heading back toward the park entrance later. "We can sit over there in the sun for a bit, on the edge of the lake."

The spot he pointed toward looked very tempting. Plus, if she were being honest with herself, she had to admit that she was reluctant for them to part ways. "All right."

They called for Peter to join them, then they stepped off the path while Georgina claimed a spot on a vacant bench. The area where they elected to sit was near the water. Worried she might get grass stains on her skirt, Emily took off her shawl and prepared to spread it across the ground.

"Allow me," said Stratton.

"It's all right. I can—" She blinked in response to the garment he'd laid out before her, then glanced at him. To her shock and dismay, he'd removed his jacket. She scanned her surroundings, hoping no one had taken notice. "You should put that back on, Your Grace. It's really not decent for you to be out and about in a state of undress."

"Do you see any more skin than usual?" She gaped at him. It was all she could do since his question had prompted all sorts of inappropriate musings. Most pressingly, would she *like* to see more?

Very much so. I'd like you to take off your shirt.

She averted her gaze on account of the heat she could feel in her cheeks. Whatever was the matter with her? This was Stratton for heaven's sake, the very same man she'd always made sure to avoid at all cost. He'd been a bothersome nuisance for years and while she'd always found him handsome and rather attractive, she'd had the good sense not to let it affect her.

Yet here she was, getting all flushed and weak-kneed, wondering what he would look like naked. It was beyond the pale. It was…It was…

"My lady?"

"Yes?" She was so startled by the sudden sound of his voice, she snapped to attention.

"I was merely saying your shawl is very light-colored. Grass stains will show. The same won't be true of my jacket." He gestured toward it. "I've deliberately turned it inside out just in case, but you can't do the same with your shawl."

"True." She sent him a hesitant glance and was instantly taken aback by how handsome he was with just a white shirt and ivory waistcoat. It accentuated his chest while affording him a very romantic, if not princely, appearance. Either way, he looked terribly dashing and she, apparently, was quite unable to turn away.

"Will you sit then?" He offered his hand to help her down and she hesitated only briefly before accepting his assistance. Strong fingers closed around hers, sending a charge up her arm. She gasped and he stilled. "Everything all right?"

"Quite so," she managed, despite the sudden dryness in her throat.

"Glad to hear it." He waited until she was comfortably seated before releasing her hand and taking a seat beside her on the grass.

"What of your breeches?" she asked. "They're also light-colored."

"No matter." He propped his arms behind him and leaned back while glancing toward the spot where Peter had taken a seat next to Heidi. The boy was grinning while Heidi persistently pushed her nose up against him. "I've got others."

"That's hardly the point."

"Isn't it?" He turned to face her, his brown eyes meeting hers with such intense pleasure she lost herself for a moment. "I'm fairly certain I have several pairs for exactly this sort of reason. So I may sacrifice one or two for the most deserving lady of my acquaintance."

She stared at him, unable to speak. Until he suddenly asked, "Why haven't you married?"

His question broke the spell and Emily managed to tear her gaze away from his. "That's a rather personal question."

"You don't have to answer if you don't want to. I'm just curious since you did have your debut six years ago. It's unusual for a lady to avoid the parson's mousetrap for so long. Especially when her father's an earl and she has an impressive dowry."

"I suppose that's true," she admitted. "Something similar could be said about you. Dukes are the ultimate prize on the marriage mart since Prince George is already taken."

Chuckling, Stratton plucked a piece of grass and fiddled with it between his fingers. "I'm beginning to understand why you kept getting in my way all the time."

"I never—"

"Admit it. You were secretly trying to trap me."

She rolled her eyes. "Yes. You've caught me. I wonder how it took you so long to realize I've always been mad about you."

"Had you torn part of your gown while falling at my feet, it might have worked." He winked and gave her a playful smile. "You're right though. Some ladies did go to great lengths in their effort to get me leg shackled, but none of their ploys met with success and none of the ladies appealed. Besides, I'm only four and twenty. I've got time."

"True." She brushed a stray strand of hair from her eyes and tucked it behind her ear.

He said nothing further and she got the impression he was waiting to see if she'd open up about her own reason for not yet tying the knot.

She couldn't. Not yet. Possibly never.

Their friendship was much too new for her to make herself that vulnerable to him.

CHAPTER SIX

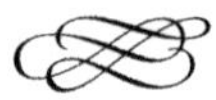

It rained for the next three days, during which Callum received no word from Lady Emily. They'd made no additional plans to meet once their walk in the park was over, and while he'd considered writing her once or twice, he'd eventually thought it best to let her decide if she wanted to see him and Peter again. The last thing he wanted to do was press her.

Standing by the parlor window, he stared at the wet street beyond. Puddles remained but the rain had ceased, giving way to a hint of sunshine that peeked from between white clouds. Was it wrong of him not to write and tell her he'd had a wonderful time?

No. He'd said so when they'd parted ways. Repeating himself in writing would only make him look desperate. He scrubbed a hand over his jaw. She was just one woman among an entire city full.

Yes, and you weren't the least bit shaken when that horse nearly ran her over.

"It's a nice day again," Peter spoke from behind him. "Can we please ask Lady Emily if we can take Heidi for a walk?"

Callum turned to face him. "I'm sorry, but I think Lady Emily ought to reach out to us next time."

Peter's face fell. "Oh."

"She's probably busy at the moment. We have to be a bit patient."

"I understand." Peter slipped from the room like a weary shadow and Callum muttered a curse.

How was it that he'd been over the moon just a few days before, only to feel like he'd now been denied the source of his future happiness? Bothered by it, he started wishing he'd never run into Lady Emily in the first place. If only Peter hadn't met Heidi, he'd not have to miss her as well.

It wasn't right. After everything he'd told her, Lady Emily ought to have written, if for no other reason than to—

"Your Grace?" Dawson, his butler, stood in the doorway. "A letter for you."

Callum snatched the missive from the salver as though it had just been tossed into a fire and he meant to save it from turning to ash. He thanked the butler and waited until he was gone before tearing the seal on the letter.

Dear Duke of Stratton,

I apologize for not getting in touch sooner, but I kept hoping the rain would cease and that I might ask you and Peter if you'd like to go for another walk. When the weather did not improve I thought to invite you both for tea yesterday. At least Peter could play with Heidi in the parlor. But then the Marchioness of Ipsly came to call together with her son. They remained for luncheon, tea, and supper which, if you ask me, was rather rude.

That aside, the weather today appears to be much improved. A walk would therefore be welcome, although I would like to make a different proposal. The paper this morning announced a fair. It's a little past Islington so it would take about an hour to get there, but I thought it might be fun for Peter. It is however worth mentioning that Heidi would have to stay home. However, if you agree, I can stop by to pick you up immediately after luncheon. Does one o'clock suit?

Should Peter prefer to spend more time with Heidi, then that's fine as well. I just thought I'd mention the fair since it will be ending in a few days.

Awaiting your response with the hope of an imminent outing,

Lady Emily Brooke.

. . .

Callum dashed from the parlor as soon as he'd finished reading the letter and ran upstairs, almost knocking a painting off the wall in his haste to find Peter. The boy was in his room when Callum entered, a little out of breath.

"I just got word," Callum said, still holding the letter in his fist. He relayed its contents and waited to see what Peter would say.

"I've never been to a fair." He looked at Callum. "I'd like to go but I'd also like to see Heidi. How do I choose?"

Callum crouched before him. "Think of it this way. The fair will end soon and, with the weather being what it is, there's no guarantee we'll be able to go tomorrow or the day after. But even if it rains, we can still stop by Rosemont House to see Heidi. Lady Emily made the suggestion herself and just to reassure you, I'll make arrangements for you to see Heidi again soon if we do go to the fair."

"Promise?"

"Absolutely."

Peter rushed at Callum and flung his arms around his neck. "Thank you."

Callum hugged the boy firmly while feeling a bit like a hero who'd just slayed a nasty dragon.

The carriage came at exactly one o'clock. Dawson announced its arrival but there was no need. Peter, who'd been watching for it from the parlor window, told Callum as soon as it pulled up in front of the door. Callum put on his hat and gloves and the pair left the house.

"Good afternoon," he said, following Peter into the carriage where Lady Emily and her maid waited. The ladies seconded the greeting, the door was pulled shut, and they were off.

Unaccustomed to travelling in a full carriage, Callum stretched out his legs without thinking and quickly pulled them back when his foot found Lady Emily's.

"Sorry." He darted a hasty look in Georgina's direction and winced in response to her chastising glance.

Lady Emily, however, did not appear to share her maid's disapproval. When Callum caught her gaze once more, she looked as though she was struggling to keep from laughing. He smiled at her. It pleased him immensely that she was seated across from him so he was able to look at her without appearing too obvious.

She pursed her lips, then shifted her feet to the right and jutted her chin in a downward direction toward her left, as if to say, *Go on. You can put your legs there.*

He glanced at the maid again and, noting she now studied the view, he decided to make himself comfortable while mouthing the words, "Thank you."

Lady Emily gave him an answering nod before

turning her attention to Peter. "I know how fond you are of Heidi, so I thought it might please you to know that I've spoken with my parents. They've both agreed you are welcome to visit whenever you like between two and five in the afternoons. Should Stratton be unable to join you, he may drop you off. In the event that I am not there, the servants will make sure you're well looked after."

Peter stared at her. So did Callum. Just when he thought the woman was done surprising him in the best way possible, she managed to do it again.

"That is extremely generous of you," Callum said when Peter failed to respond.

He nudged the boy who suddenly blinked. "Yes. Thank you ever so much."

"My pleasure." Lady Emily smiled at him with affection. "Now tell me what you'd most like to see at the fair. It's my understanding that there are jugglers, acrobats, and various animals. The advertisement even mentioned pleasure boats as well as up-and-downs."

Her question gave way to an animated discussion. Peter was very intrigued by the mention of acrobats and wanted to know what sort of acts they might be performing.

Lady Emily grinned. "We'll have to see, but I'm sure they'll be good at balancing on their hands. I once saw one walk across a rope strung high between two poles."

"How is such a thing possible?" Peter asked, his voice filled with awe.

"With vast amounts of practice, I imagine," Callum said with a chuckle. He shifted his legs and stilled when they came to rest against Lady Emily's. When she didn't move, neither did he, though his pulse did leap and his stomach contracted.

"Practice is important," Lady Emily murmured, still not moving her legs.

Callum darted a quick look in her direction, but her gaze remained on Peter. Had she even noticed they were touching? He'd no idea, but he hoped so since that surely meant she liked the closeness as much as he.

The possibility of such an occurrence danced through the air with the promise of something exquisite. He froze while the conversation continued around him. Of all the people in the world, he never would have expected to forge a bond with Lady Emily, yet here he was, happy with the intimacy they shared in this moment.

The carriage came to a halt and his thoughts on the matter scattered. Leaning forward, he opened the door so they could alight, ever conscious of the fact that she was becoming more important to him with each passing second.

The atmosphere at the fair was brimming with energy. It felt like all of London was eager to get out after the rain and had chosen to spend the afternoon here. Emily glanced around as they pressed their way through the crowd. A group of musicians who stood upon a raised platform were playing a lively tune with their fiddles.

Farther ahead was a tent with a sign that read, *Hall of Mirrors*. Another one promised a magical show while a third claimed it contained a collection of the bizarre.

"Look," said Peter. "That man's blowing fire."

They stopped to watch and Stratton tossed a few coins into the man's hat before moving on.

"This was a splendid idea," he told her when they'd seen a bear perform a balancing act while a monkey played a trumpet. "Peter is having a marvelous time."

What about you, she wanted to ask, only to shy away from the question. It felt too obvious, even though her decision to let his legs rest against hers in the carriage was even more so. She should have avoided the contact, but the discreet intimacy it had provided made her feel closer to him somehow, and she'd liked that.

"As am I," she said, deciding to let him know she was glad to have made the suggestion. Raising her voice she asked Peter, "Shall we try to catch the next magic act?"

"Oh yes. Let's."

Peter started toward the tent but Stratton caught his hand. "Stay close. It's a large crowd and I don't want to lose you."

Emily made sure Georgina was following close behind too before falling into step beside Stratton. When they reached the tent, Emily already had several coins at the ready.

"You did say I could pay the next time," she told Stratton when he looked ready to protest.

He flattened his mouth, took a deep breath, and finally nodded, then gestured for her to precede him. She paid the fee and entered the tent where chairs stood in three long rows. Deciding a spot at the front would be best if Peter was to have a good view, she made her way toward the end of that row where a few spots remained vacant.

Arriving first, she claimed the seat farthest away while Stratton, who'd entered behind her with Peter, sat down beside her with the boy positioned between the duke and Georgina.

Emily kept her gaze carefully trained on the spot where she expected the magician to appear, but try as she might, she could not stop from wondering about their seating arrangement. Had he selected the chair next to hers on purpose? If so, why? What did it mean?

She shook her head. How silly she was being. In all likelihood, he'd merely taken the first available seat he'd arrived at. But why not suggest Peter sit between them? Or Georgina, for that matter?

Good grief. She'd drive herself mad if she kept cross examining every decision he made.

"I saw a bakery stand near the entrance with tables and benches in front," Stratton told her. The length of his arm pressed against hers as he shifted closer. "Perhaps we can have a hot drink and some cake there after the performance. My treat."

"Mmm…hmm…"

What else was she to say when the scent of him wafted around her? Lord, he smelled good – of sandalwood, fresh mint, and something exclusively him. Why hadn't she noticed before? Perhaps because she'd been too busy cursing the constant disruption he'd brought to her life.

How foolish she'd been. How unfair and unkind.

"Ladies and gentlemen," a short and plump man announced. "Prepare to be amazed by the extraordinary, the marvelous, and the unique. I bring to you, the one and only, Jimmy Fortuno!"

Everyone cheered as a cloud of smoke appeared behind the announcer. And again when it faded to reveal a slim man dressed in black and scarlet. He proceeded to turn a collection of handkerchiefs into a bouquet of flowers before moving on to a series of card tricks. Most impressive, was a disappearing act involving a rabbit.

Throughout it all, Emily's attention remained on

the man beside her. Whenever he clapped, his elbow brushed hers, and as he angled himself to speak with Peter, she felt the press of his knee against her own.

By the time the performance was over, she was so hot and flustered over the impact he was having on her, she could barely breathe. What she needed was copious amounts of fresh air. Annoyingly, she noticed, he seemed perfectly fine. Nothing about him suggested he might be in need of smelling salts on account of *her* presence.

This made her curious. In the past, he'd always seemed slightly out of sorts whenever they'd come into contact. This well-composed version of him was something new altogether. She wasn't entirely sure how to handle him not being clumsy and was almost relieved when he spilled the tea he'd ordered for her at the bakery booth a short while later.

He managed to pull back just in time to stop it from scalding her hand.

"Sorry." The smile that followed was slightly bashful. "I mustn't forget to be careful around you."

She thanked him for the tea and sipped it while Peter dug into the chocolate cake he'd been given. Georgina, who sat to Emily's right, was enjoying a scone. Stratton, who'd sat down across from Emily, was just about to take a sip of his coffee when something seemed to draw his attention.

He raised his hand and waved while sending

someone a grin. Emily turned and saw Anthony and his wife, Ada.

"I see you had the same idea as us," Anthony said with a wide smile.

Greetings were exchanged before Ada said, "We just arrived and thought we'd try to catch the next magic show. Have you seen it?"

"Yes," said Peter. "It was marvelous. The magician was able to make an entire rabbit disappear inside his top hat."

"That does sound impressive," said Ada. She turned to Emily and told her softly, "I'm thrilled to see you here."

The comment was followed by a wry smile and a very pointed look in Stratton's direction.

Emily shook her head. "It's not what you think."

"Isn't it?" Ada pursed her lips. Humor danced in her eyes. Before Emily had a chance to respond, Ada asked, "How's your reading coming along?"

"Very well. I should be able to start on the book you gave me within a few days."

"Thank you again for doing me this favor."

"It's hardly a favor, Ada. Had I known you'd written a novel I would have begged you to let me read it anyway."

"You're a good friend." Ada sent Stratton another glance before telling Emily, "Enjoy the rest of your outing." She and Anthony said their goodbyes and wandered off in the direction of the magician's tent.

"They think there's more than friendship between us," Stratton told her a short while later when they were walking back to the carriage.

Emily nearly tripped. "Who does?"

She didn't need to ask, but her question did help her stall for the time she required to adjust to his comment.

"Anthony and Ada." Stratton, she saw, kept his attention on the direction in which they were headed. It almost looked as though he'd not spoken to her at all.

"Ridiculous," she muttered, not daring to give away even the slightest hint of how he made her feel. Just in case he remained unaffected by her. He'd already told her that none of the ladies he'd met appealed in the way of marriage. Not that she was thinking that far ahead, but surely his statement included her. Didn't it?

"I couldn't agree with you more," he said, confirming her fear.

The attraction and overall wish for something more than what they presently shared was completely one-sided.

How utterly perfect. The situation wasn't improved by the fact that she'd likely be seeing a great deal more of him now that she'd made her home available to Peter every afternoon. Stratton would probably join him for the most part, forcing her to spend additional time with a man she'd started thinking about a lot more than what was wise.

Peter and Georgina entered the carriage first, then Stratton caught hold of Emily's hand. Her eyes met his and she saw something there – some deeply buried emotion she failed to define. It was gone in an instant and he was handing her up.

She took her seat on the bench while he claimed the opposite spot next to Peter. This time, however, he kept his legs bent at the knees. He did not stretch them out and let them touch hers, despite her wishing with all her heart that he would.

CHAPTER SEVEN

Of all the situations Callum had thought he'd find himself in, this wasn't one of them.

He stared at his reflection in the cheval glass once he'd finished dressing. If someone had told him just two weeks ago that he would be losing his heart to Emily Brooke, he'd have laughed. Yet here he was, utterly smitten while she remained completely indifferent to him.

She'd said as much, hadn't she, when he'd mentioned Anthony thinking there might be more than friendship between them.

Ridiculous, was the word she'd used.

He sighed and unwound his cravat for the third time. If only he'd not had to sack his valet, but alas, Mr. Jones had been one of the highest paid servants and one of the few Callum could manage without.

He made another attempt at the knot and decided it would have to do.

"Can we please visit Rosemont House today?" Peter asked when Callum met him for breakfast.

Callum stared at the paper he'd been pretending to read. "Maybe tomorrow."

"That's what you told me yesterday," Peter grumbled. "And the day before."

It was, Callum admitted, what he'd been telling the poor boy for the past week. He set the paper aside so he could give him his full attention. "I'm sorry, but I've been busy."

No. You've been a coward.

Peter stared at him. "She *did* say you could just drop me off. You don't have to stay."

Of course the boy would remember that. Callum attempted a placating smile. "My mother has a spaniel. I can ask her if we can stop by for a visit later this week. What do you think of that?"

Peter shrugged one shoulder. "It won't be the same."

Of course it wouldn't. They'd have to deal with Mama for one thing. She'd married an artist after Papa's death and had since become an eccentric. The fact that he'd rather visit her than go anywhere near Rosemont House spoke volumes.

It might have been different had Lady Emily written to him after the fair, but he'd had no word from her since. The future of their friendship, or whatever this thing they'd embarked upon was, had been placed in his hands. He could either act or do nothing.

Knowing what he should do, which was to put Peter first, didn't help.

"Very well," he said upon reflection, "I'll take you there after luncheon."

Peter bounced up and down in his chair, his excitement so infectious Callum could not keep from laughing.

"Thank you ever so much!"

Callum dipped his chin and returned his attention to the paper. He'd leave Peter at Rosemont House for a couple of hours while visiting Brody who lived nearby. What he would not do, was spend additional time with Lady Emily. Distance was required now if he was to stop thinking of her all the time. It was also imperative that he get his incessant desire to kiss her under control. He reasoned this would be easier to do if he didn't spend time with her.

As had so often been the case during the course of their acquaintance, however, luck was not on his side. The moment the Rosemont butler opened the door, there she was, having just descended the stairs to the foyer.

Wonderful.

It didn't help that she looked divine with her red curls pinned in a slightly wild updo that left some stray locks falling softly around her face. The pleasure in her eyes when she saw who'd come to call, only added to her incredible beauty.

"You're here," she muttered as though incredulous.

"We are," Callum said.

When nothing further was added by either one, the butler asked, "Will Your Grace be coming inside?"

"Oh...um...I actually—"

"Please do."

Emily's voice, and the hopefulness it conveyed, made him forget all about the distance he'd planned on putting between them. His feet stepped forward and he entered the house together with Peter.

"It's good to see you again," Lady Emily said once they'd arrived in the parlor.

They sat exactly as they had on his previous visit, only this time Peter was here as well. He sat on the floor, playing with Heidi. A tea tray had been placed on the table before them.

"You too." He watched as she gracefully filled each of their cups and wondered what it might be like to have those elegant fingers slide over his skin. A hot shiver raked his spine and his muscles tightened. Best he avoid such musings if he was to keep his body under control.

"I realize it's silly, but I really must ask." She'd

lowered her voice to a whisper. "Did I say or do something to offend you when last we met?"

Her question caught him completely off guard. "Of course not. Why would you think so?"

"It's nothing. Forget I mentioned it." The smile that followed looked slightly forced. Callum cursed himself. In staying away, he'd apparently given the wrong impression. He tried to think of a way to reassure her, but before he could find the right words, she asked, "So what have the two of you been doing this past week?"

"Nothing much," Peter said. He jutted his chin toward Callum. "He's been busy."

"I see." Lady Emily smoothed her skirt over her knees. "Hopefully with something more fun than tending to estate matters."

He relaxed in response to the sly gleam that lit up her eyes when she met his gaze. This teasing banter felt better – more like them – comfortable and relaxing. "Unfortunately not. How about you?"

She took a deep breath. "The Earl of Millfield stopped by the day before last. He came without his mother this time and thankfully refrained from staying longer than an hour."

"A potential suitor?" Callum forced the words out from behind gritted teeth. He'd not spared Millfield much thought when Lady Emily mentioned him stopping by with his mother. But if he'd returned without the marchioness, his intentions were clear.

"Mama and Papa have insisted I take him seriously but the very thought of living with him for the rest of my life is very off-putting." She shook her head. "As expected, Mama and Papa would like to see me married. Thankfully, they also desire to see me happy, which is why they've assured me they won't force my hand."

"So you intend to deny Millfield the chance to court you?"

"It's already done."

Callum breathed a sigh of relief. "Good. I believe you made the correct decision."

She gave him a puzzled look and it occurred to him that he might have revealed too much.

"Really?" she asked.

He cleared his throat. "I mean, you obviously weren't very keen on the man. After managing to avoid marriage as long as you have, it would be a shame for you to wed for the sake of wedding alone."

Heidi yapped with playful enthusiasm and Peter's responding laughter drew Lady Emily's attention away from Callum for a second. She smiled, then collected her teacup, and said, "Marriage is the done thing. I believe that's the primary incentive for most people."

"It won't be mine," he told her without really thinking.

Her gaze snapped to his. She tilted her head and

her expression, which had been curious at first, gave way to surprise. "You want a love match?"

"My mother has married for love twice now, so I know it's possible." When all she did was stare at him as though he'd just arrived from a different planet, he asked, "Are your parents aware that you and I have been spending time together?"

"Yes." She drank from her cup as though she were trying to hide behind it.

This was interesting.

Could it be that he had misinterpreted her response toward him? Was it possible she might have more of an interest in him than he had believed? What if she was just as afraid of rejection as he was?

It was a topic that warranted exploration.

"And have they not questioned the reason for this?"

Her cheeks turned a deep shade of pink. She lowered her teacup and brushed some invisible fuzz from her skirt. "They asked if we were courting. I told them we weren't. Which is true. Is it not?"

"It is," he confirmed, for what else could he say?

"We're friends, you and I." Her gaze was suddenly so intense it pierced him to the core. "I would never attempt to trap you, Your Grace. I like you too well to force you into a marriage of convenience with me."

He didn't like what her comment implied. The

idea that she believed they'd be unhappy together was more upsetting than he'd thought possible. "I see."

Needing to shift his thoughts to something besides Lady Emily and the havoc she'd brought to his very existence, Callum excused himself and went to join Peter. He didn't care if it was considered improper for a duke to lie on the floor while a boy and a dog took turns leaping over his legs. All that mattered was the distraction it offered, however fleeting he knew it would be.

Emily watched Stratton play with Peter and Heidi while trying to pinpoint the moment when everything had gone sideways. They'd had a wonderful walk in the park, a lovely trip to the fair, and now this. Her heart sank. It felt as though there was an ocean between them and she couldn't figure out why.

Again she wondered if she might have said something wrong.

She snatched up a biscuit and frowned while she ate it. His entire demeanor had changed when she'd mentioned not wanting to force him into a marriage of convenience. But hadn't he just denied that there was anything more between them than friendship?

Had he wished to, he could have hinted at their

outings potentially leading to courtship. Instead he'd confirmed a lack of interest in venturing down that path with her. She'd worried he might have taken her comment the wrong way and so, she'd said what she'd said.

If only she were brave enough to tell him how she felt and then deal with the chance that he might reject her. It would save her from constantly wondering over his words and the intonation with which he spoke, from analyzing the look in his eyes when he glanced at her, and the meaning behind the occasional touch.

She reached for her tea while wishing for a way to figure him out.

"Would you like to visit again tomorrow?" she asked when he and Peter prepared to leave.

"I'd love to," Peter said, only for Stratton to give him a chastising frown.

"Thank you for the invitation," said Stratton. "I'll ask one of the footmen to bring Peter over."

"Oh." Emily stared at him while her heart quietly broke. He was turning her down. It couldn't be clearer. She tried to smile but didn't quite manage. "You won't be joining him then?"

"I'm afraid I can't afford to."

They departed, leaving Emily behind with an awfully hollow sensation behind her breastbone.

"Is something troubling you?" Ada asked when

Emily joined her and Harriet for tea a few days later. "You seem distracted again."

"It's nothing," Emily assured her while doing her best to feign happiness.

"You also look tired," Harriet said. "Have you not been sleeping well?"

"If you must know, I've been staying up later than usual in order to finish the book I'm currently reading."

Ada smirked. "Are you sure it's the book that's keeping you from your sleep?"

"Do you know something I don't?" Harriet asked. She sent Ada a curious look.

"Only that Anthony and I saw Emily with Stratton last week. They were at the fair together."

"Were they really?" Harriet's eyes had widened to the size of saucers. She shifted her attention back to Emily, giving her an expectant look.

Emily waved one hand in the hope of dismissing whatever suspicions her friends might have. "Stratton's ward, Peter, lost his parents earlier this year. He's been struggling with the mourning process. When I realized he'd taken an instant liking to Heidi, I suggested a walk so the two could spend more time together."

"At the fair?" Harriet asked.

"No, this was prior to that."

"So you've had several outings with Stratton," Ada remarked.

"*And* Peter," Emily pointed out. "Don't give me that look. It was not several outings. It was two. Three if we count the walk. Plus a couple of visits for tea. As well as some letters. And a bouquet of flowers."

She added the last part when both of her friends raised their eyebrows at the mention of letters and instantly regretted it when they began grinning like fools.

"Oh, Emily." Ada reached for her hand and gave it a squeeze. "I'm delighted on your behalf."

Emily gave her a wary look. "What are you talking about?"

Ada glanced at Harriet. "She truly can't see it, can she?"

Harriet shook her head while looking much too amused for Emily's liking. "I don't believe so."

"You're being courted." Ada grinned. "And you don't even know it."

"No, I…I'm really not. Stratton and I are friends, Ada. That's it. Nothing more."

"If I were to hazard a guess, it's not a book that has you distracted. It's him. Isn't it?"

"He's not courting me," Emily told them both firmly. "He made that much abundantly clear."

"But you'd like him to," Harriet murmured. "Am I right?"

"I…" Emily slumped. "What good does *that* do when he doesn't want the same?"

"You say he brought you flowers?" When Emily nodded in response to Ada's question, she asked, "What kind?"

"It was an original bouquet. Very colorful."

"So he took time putting some thought into it."

"I suppose. But only because I was clear about not wanting roses." She shook her head. "He and I have always been at odds. We've a history of disastrous encounters with each other. To be honest, I didn't think I'd ever enjoy spending time with him at all."

"But you do," Harriet said with a soft smile.

Emily nodded. "I must confess, I miss him when we're apart. Unfortunately, our last meeting didn't go well. He made no indication that he'd want to see me again when he left, so it's fairly obvious to me that he does not feel the same as I do."

"I think you're mistaken," Harriet said. When Emily gave her a dubious look, she explained, "He's a duke, Emily. He's aware of social rules and etiquette. If he wrote you letters, brought you flowers, walked with you in the park *and* took you to a fair while meeting you for tea in between, the man most assuredly has an interest in more than friendship with you."

"It was for Peter's benefit," Emily told them. "He's the reason Stratton got in touch with me in the first place."

"Don't be daft, Emily. Had that been the case

there would not have been flowers. He'd have sent a maid with the boy for all those excursions, but he didn't, did he?" When Emily shook her head, Harriet said, "Peter wants to spend time with Heidi, and that gave Stratton the chance to spend time with you."

"I..." Emily blinked. Could that be true?

"He's more reserved than Anthony and Brody," Ada told Emily. "I doubt he'd reveal his affection for you unless he was certain of your affection for him."

The conversation gave Emily much to consider once her friends left. She took care not to let herself get too excited in case they were wrong. Instead, she re-read the letters he'd sent her and thought back on their interactions, all while searching for clues. Eventually, she gave up in favor of reading, no wiser now than she'd been that morning. If anything, she was much more confused.

And then the letter from Seaton Hall arrived the next morning, announcing an unexpected decline in her grandmother's health.

"Have the carriage readied," Papa told Larrow. "We'll depart as soon as we've finished breaking our fast."

"Will you join us?" Mama asked Emily. Her voice cracked just enough to reveal what a terrible blow this was to her. She and her mother had always been close. With the viscountess not yet older than five and sixty, the idea she might soon die had come as a shock.

"Of course," Emily promised. She loved Grandmama dearly and couldn't imagine not saying goodbye. "I'll go and ready myself."

They set off within the hour and made good time with the team of six horses Papa had requested. The journey took little more than an hour before the estate where Mama had grown up came into view. Emily had last visited over the summer, during which Grandmama had appeared to be in excellent health. She'd served them lemonade on the terrace and had even engaged in a game of pall mall with Emily and her cousins. She'd also come to London once a month since then so she could participate in the book club Emily ran.

Sadly, the woman Emily found when Grandpapa showed them all to her Grandmama's chamber, bore no resemblance to the energetic woman Emily had known. In her place was someone so frail she didn't appear to have the strength required to last the night.

It was the most heartbreaking thing Emily had ever witnessed.

Mama choked back a sob as she went to her mother's bedside. She perched there on the edge of the mattress and clasped her slim hand.

Apparently, a fit of some sort had occurred the previous evening. As a result, Grandmama could no longer move the left side of her body. Her speech was unclear, and the attending physicians were not optimistic. They claimed it had put a terrible strain on her heart.

"She'd like to speak with you," Mama told Emily once she was finished.

Emily swallowed and approached the bed at a slow tread. If only Stratton were here with her now, supporting her as he'd done when he'd saved her from that horse. She needed him in this moment if only to tell her that she could get through this and that he'd be there for her after.

Having reached the bed, she did what she could to stay strong for Grandmama's sake. It would not do for her to break down in tears, yet keeping them at bay was a struggle. Her eyes stung and a painful knot had formed in her throat.

"You…mustn't…weep," Grandmama murmured while slurring each word. "It's…life. Love…and… loss. Can't have one with…without the other."

"It's much too soon," Emily croaked. Leaning forward, she hugged the older woman while taking care not to hurt her. The tears she spilled dampened the sheets. "I'm not ready to let you go."

"These shifts in life…will be easier…once you marry. My only regret. Not a single grandchild wed."

Emily straightened so she could meet her grandmother's gaze. "It's not so simple."

"You just…need to find the right man." The bleakness in Grandmama's eyes was distressing. "You should have…done so by now."

Troubled by the energy Grandmama seemed to require to get the words out, Emily tried to convince her to rest, but the old woman would hear nothing of it. Her eyes had sharpened and though she looked like she lay at death's door, it was clear now that she had a final battle to win before she made her departure.

"Think of the future," she pressed. "Time…is fleeting. You're… two-and-twenty…but you've never been courted."

"That's not true," Emily blurted for no other purpose than to appease an old woman and give her some peace. "I…I'm being courted right now."

Grandmama snorted. "There's no need to lie just to...make me happy."

"I'm not lying," Emily told her, digging herself into deeper trouble. "In fact, I'm fairly sure I'm about to become engaged."

What was the harm in giving an old woman joy?

"To whom?" Grandmama asked with interest.

Emily didn't hesitate. "The Duke of Stratton."

"Ha." The old woman actually managed what looked like a tiny laugh, if the twitch at the edge of her mouth was anything to go by. "He's not…the marrying sort."

"People change," Emily insisted.

Grandmama merely sighed. "Forgive me. All this…talking has worn me out. I…need to rest."

"Of course." Emily gave her hand a squeeze and

dropped a kiss to her brow. She then retreated from her grandmother's bedside. When she met one of the doctors outside in the hallway, she asked, "How long do you think she has left?"

"It's hard to say. Could be as much as a couple of weeks or as little as two or three days. Depends on her will to live, I suppose."

Emily nodded as those words sank in. If the doctor was right, she might just have enough time to fulfill her grandmother's dying wish.

CHAPTER EIGHT

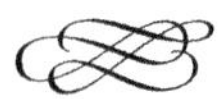

Callum gaped at Lady Emily, who sat before him, quietly waiting for his response. The message he'd received from her last night had mentioned an urgent matter. She'd requested he call upon her the following morning, at his earliest convenience. So he'd set off for Rosemont House as soon as it was appropriate for him to do so, and was now comfortably seated in the parlor.

Naturally, he'd been concerned. And worried. He'd hardly slept since he'd tried to work out what this was about. But he'd not imagined this.

"You want me to do what?"

He still couldn't quite comprehend her request. She'd spoken in a rush while clutching her hands and strolling about in a state of complete agitation. Finally, she'd ceased her pacing and lowered herself to a spot on the sofa. Her eyes were wide, imploring pools of green.

"I realize it sounds a bit mad, but you are the only person who might be willing to help."

"By lying to your grandmother?" He just wanted to be perfectly clear about what she was asking of him.

"Is it so terribly wrong if it lets her die happy?" Lady Emily gazed back at him as though he had the means by which to save the entire kingdom if only he'd try. When he didn't answer – not because he had nothing to say but because there were too many thoughts filling his brain – she shook her head. "I'm sorry. It's a silly idea. Let's forget I asked."

"I beg your pardon?" He stared at her. "You've just asked that I pretend to be your fiancé, and now you want me to forget it?"

"I'm sure you have more pressing matters to attend to than this and judging from your response, you're not inclined to do it. Which I completely understand. Honestly, I don't know what I was thinking."

He was fairly certain he did. She loved her grandmother and was attempting to fulfill her dying wish. That was precisely the sort of lovely thing he'd expect from her, the only problem being all the potential complications that might arise while carrying out the plan.

He took a deep breath and slowly expelled it.

"First of all, I'd like to take a moment to tell you how sorry I am to hear of your grandmother's grave condition. That cannot be easy for you or your parents."

She averted her gaze briefly, but not enough to hide the tears that welled in her eyes. It tore at his heart knowing she suffered – that she would soon suffer more when news of her grandmother's death arrived. Dismissing propriety, he reached for her hand. She started a little, but quickly relaxed and allowed him to simply offer the comfort he wished to impart.

"I am your friend." It was imperative he make that clear. Even if he had a burning desire to be something more, his primary goal at the moment was offering strength and support. "I'm also glad that you felt able to come to me with this request. It caught me by surprise, that's all. I hadn't expected an offer of marriage when I left my home this morning."

He added a teasing smile. The truth was, she had completely swept the rug from under his feet.

"It was very bold of me, I'll admit." Gratitude shone in her eyes, and Callum's heart melted.

"So just to be sure I understand, you wish for us to visit your grandmother together. Yes?" She'd related the details too quickly for him to follow. His mind had been stuck on 'pretend courtship'.

She nodded. "Grandmama didn't believe me

when I told her you and I were courting. She… doesn't believe you to be the marrying sort, I'm afraid."

"Hmm…" He reflected on that a moment. Marrying wasn't something he'd spent much time thinking about, until recently As he'd told Lady Emily, he had time. But when he was with her, he felt the uncanny need for something more permanent. It was a feeling unlike any other and one he feared she did not share.

This complicated her request since a small part of him secretly wished for it to be real. If he weren't careful, he could end up brokenhearted, but wasn't that a risk worth taking if he truly cared about her?

"Your grandmother isn't wrong," he said. "I've shown no interest in courtship or marriage before. In fact, the first lady I've called on with flowers is you."

Her eyes widened. "Really?"

His heart beat a bit harder at the realization that she seemed to like that idea.

Careful.

He released her hand and positioned himself with his forearms resting upon his thighs and his hands clasped together. "No one else can know about this."

"Does that mean you'll do it?"

It was a big request, but why should he refuse?

He had no other attachment and he did owe her a favor for helping him out with Peter.

He gave his consent before he could change his mind. "Yes."

"Thank you." The relief with which she spoke assured him he'd made the right decision. This would not only give Viscountess Seaton peace. It would also give it to Lady Emily.

Still, the endeavor was not without risk. He had to make that clear to her. "If word gets out that you and I travelled to visit your grandmother's deathbed together, assumptions will be made."

"Agreed." She nodded with the keenness of an adventuress about to explore an unchartered land. "I thought we might meet somewhere along the way and continue onward from there."

He tried to think of a discreet location. "There's a church in Camden, near the main road. Do you know it?"

"No, but I'm sure my coachman does."

There was another detail that needed addressing. "I trust Georgina will be joining us?"

"Of course. My reputation will be preserved."

He was pleased to hear it. "And when would you like to depart?"

"Today. As early as possible since Mama and Papa intend to return to Seaton Hall themselves this evening. I'd like to go and come back before then."

"Very well. I'll need to return home first, but I

can meet you at the designated spot in a couple of hours. Will that do?"

"Yes."

He stood, gave a short bow, and departed, all the while wondering what the hell he'd just gotten into. It wasn't until he'd already set off that he realized how problematic this could become for them both.

Making big decisions with haste was always unwise and he had to admit, this plan he'd agreed to help Lady Emily with, was no small thing. He should have taken more time to consider the possible implications it could potentially lead to. But with a viscountess on her deathbed, he hadn't.

Instead he'd agreed, not taking into account that Lady Emily's grandfather would have to be informed of their courtship as well. Callum doubted the viscount would go along with deceiving his wife, so they would have to lie to him too. Which pretty much ensured this would all spiral out of control.

Two hours later, Callum muttered a curse as he climbed from his hired carriage. He walked to the spot where the Rosemont carriage was meant to pick him up and glanced at his pocket watch. Five to eleven. She'd be here any minute.

No sooner had he returned the watch to his jacket pocket, than he spotted the carriage. It wasn't the same one she'd used when they'd gone to the fair. This one was unmarked, he noted.

It pulled to a stop and Callum greeted the coachman before climbing in.

"Good day, ladies," he said, by way of greeting as he settled onto the bench opposite Lady Emily and her maid. "A pleasure to see you again."

"Thank you for coming." Lady Emily wore a somber expression, but that didn't stop her from smiling at him with what looked like genuine pleasure.

"How could I refuse?" He winked at her and pulled the door shut, then knocked on the roof.

The carriage jolted into motion, rolling toward their next destination, which Lady Emily claimed to be just one hour away. Callum watched her while trying to think of something to say. The subject he wished to broach would have to wait since he'd no idea how much Lady Emily might have revealed to her maid.

He drummed his fingers against his thigh and suddenly thought of a different means by which to pass the time. "Shall we exchange this or that questions?"

"As a means by which to discover our differences and similarities?"

"Precisely." He stopped drumming his fingers and tilted his head. "I'll give you an easy one to start with. Day or night?"

"I've always been a day person."

"Me too." He smiled at her softly and saw that the tightness in her features was starting to ease. "Your turn."

"Very well." She folded her hands in her lap. "Red or white wine."

"Red." He didn't even have to think about it. "And you?"

"Also red."

The edge of his mouth quirked. "Town or country?"

"That's a tough one, but I suppose if I had to choose I'd probably pick the town. As much as I love the country, I always end up missing the bookshops and the theatre."

"I wasn't aware you enjoyed the theatre."

"Doesn't everyone?" She grinned and he was delighted to have distracted her from the ache he knew she felt in her breast at the moment. "I think that brings me to the next question. Ballet or opera?"

"As I'm sure you can appreciate, I'm not very fond of dancing."

"No?" Her eyes sparkled. "I wonder why."

"Minx." She looked quite pretty with her sage green bonnet and matching velvet spencer. His gaze dropped to her lips, so perfectly pink and lush. God, how he'd love to kiss her. He cleared his throat and forced his eyes to meet hers while telling her softly, "You're the only lady I've ever danced with."

It was a telling confession. He'd no idea why he'd brought it up.

"Because of what happened?"

He nodded. "I was horrified by how badly it went and feared another attempt, so I haven't danced since."

"We'll have to rectify that."

He gave her a dubious look. "How?"

"By having another go at it of course. How else?"

"Absolutely not." If there was one thing he wouldn't do, it was dance with her again.

She huffed a breath and flattened her mouth in a frustrated sort of way. "Dancing can be enjoyable. You cannot honestly mean to go through the rest of your life without making further attempts."

"I've managed well enough so far."

A frown puckered her brow. "As we've already established, you weren't the only one who got the steps wrong that day. I made mistakes too."

"Yes, but *you* didn't crush my toes." He pinched the bridge of his nose and sighed. Perhaps it was time to address the past and put it to rest once and for all. "The truth is, I was anxious."

"I gathered as much," she said with a chuckle, "though I cannot imagine why. You were one of the most sought-after bachelors London had to offer."

"A fact that did little to reduce the pressure of getting everything right. And then you came along."

"Me?"

"I knew the moment I saw you that I was in trouble. My face got all hot and my hands started sweating. It honestly felt like I might be sick."

"How flattering," she muttered, looking slightly affronted.

"You made me so bloody nervous," he added before he could change his mind.

Her lips parted. She shook her head as if baffled. "I don't see how. Was it something I said or—"

"It was simply you." He held her gaze while letting that statement sink in. "I'd never seen a lady more dazzling. You made me feel self-conscious for the first time in my life."

"But…I am the furthest thing from what is considered classically pretty. My hair is red instead of fashionably blonde. I'm also unusually tall for a woman and—"

"You're perfect, my lady. Don't ever let anyone tell you otherwise."

"I…" Her mouth opened and closed a few times but no additional words came.

Callum glanced at the maid. It bothered him that she'd overheard their exchange, but he also felt much lighter now that he'd told Lady Emily of the effect she'd had on him from the beginning. He'd never told anyone else. Papa had just thought he was horsing about and had scolded him for it later.

"Strawberry shortcake or trifle?" he asked.

"Sorry?"

"For dessert," Callum clarified. "What's your preference?"

"Oh…um…strawberry shortcake I suppose." When she said nothing more, he nudged her foot. "Your turn."

"Right. Of course. Um… Pall mall or billiards?"

"Pall mall, I should think."

The smile that followed was one of surprise and wonder. "It would seem we have a great deal in common."

His gaze caught hers. "Mind if I stretch out my legs?"

Something incredibly tempting flashed in those pretty eyes of hers. A flush rose to her cheeks and he wished with all his heart that it was because she was starting to want him as much as he wanted her.

"By all means," she said, her manner so breezy it gave no hint of being the least bit affected by what he'd asked.

She turned to address her maid, bringing up something about some trim she wished to apply to one of her gowns. Her legs moved, allowing Callum the space he needed. He pushed his feet forward between Lady Emily's feet and the wall of the carriage, and crossed his legs at the ankles.

The conversation about the trim ended and Lady Emily shifted back into position while moving her skirts as if trying to get more comfortable. The voluminous fabric fell over Callum's feet, and then her ankles pressed against his.

A rush of desire heated his veins. His pulse quickened and his breath caught. Having crossed his arms, he dug his fingertips into his biceps while staring toward the spot where he and Lady Emily touched. Although he couldn't see them, he knew her stocking-clad ankles rested against his boots.

His muscles tightened and he directed a hasty glance toward the maid, whose attention was now on the view. Had she not been here, Callum had little doubt that he would have dragged Lady Emily into his lap and kissed her senseless.

There was a reason why young ladies needed chaperones. To protect them from men with wicked intentions. And frankly, his intentions toward Lady Emily were becoming increasingly so. Oh, he could deny it as much as he wished, but that didn't change the fact that he'd wondered about her on several occasions.

Apparently, the better he got to know her, the lustier his thoughts became.

He swept his gaze back to the lady in question and saw that she studied him with open interest.

"Are you more comfortable now, Your Grace?" There was a hint of mischief to her voice that instantly filled his head with all sorts of lascivious ideas. Good Lord. This had to end.

"Perfectly so," he murmured while doing his best

not to wonder how long it would take to work through the buttons that ran down the front of her spencer. "Thank you."

She dipped her head and said nothing further, but her gaze remained locked with his until they reached their destination.

CHAPTER NINE

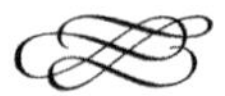

What on earth was she doing?

Emily hadn't a clue. All she knew was that she'd been completely bowled over by Stratton's confession about her making him nervous. It was hard to believe she was able to have such a potent effect on anyone. But it had made her think over all of their previous encounters in greater detail.

What if his face hadn't grown red with anger as she'd always believed, but rather because he'd been flustered?

She thought that adorable if it were true, though she'd never dare tell him as much.

Add to this the manner in which he'd held her after saving her in Hyde Park, the occasional touches he'd delivered while at the fair, and the distance he'd put between them after she had suggested a marriage between them would not be a love match but rather one of convenience.

All of it reminded her of Ada's and Harriet's words.

Perhaps they were right.

Maybe Stratton did have an interest in her beyond simply having her help him with Peter. And if so, wasn't it worth exploring when she herself had recently realized she wanted more than friendship from him?

Wasn't this what had caused her to come up with this insane idea of a fake courtship to start with? So they could play-act a little and maybe let their true feelings show?

It was all meant to be very proper of course. No impassioned lapses in judgement to put them at risk of actually *having* to marry. Unless they chose to.

If Stratton proposed, she wanted it to be from the heart.

The first part of her plan, to discover if he might be open to more than friendship with her, had presented itself when he'd asked to stretch out his legs. She'd imagined it might be like last time: comfortably reassuring.

However, she'd not anticipated his response, never mind the effect it had upon *her*.

With just one look, he'd turned her into a woman intent on seduction, even though she hadn't the foggiest clue how to do it. Somehow, by simply responding to him, she'd figured it out though. If the heated look in his eyes was any indication.

She gripped her reticule firmly in her lap and stared straight ahead, at the man who sat before her, looking much like he tried to undress her with his gaze. Heat swept the back of her neck and her pulse quickened to such an extent it rendered her breathless.

The edge of his mouth rose with smug satisfaction, as though he knew precisely what he was doing to her and how needy it made her. Heavens, she actually wanted to pull him toward her and press her mouth to his.

Thank goodness Georgina was with her to stop her from being so brash.

The carriage began to slow. It pulled up in front of Seaton Hall's entrance moments later. The door was opened and the steps set down. Stratton alit and turned so he could assist her. Their fingers touched, sending a jolt up her arm. She gasped, missed the next step, and fell.

A strong arm caught her and pulled her upright. She reached for support until her palm came to rest on a muscular chest. Tilting her head back, she stared into Stratton's captivating eyes and saw temptation.

His hold on her tightened a smidgen. It seemed his throat worked as he swallowed.

"My lady," he murmured right before easing her gently away and adding appropriate distance.

He helped Georgina next before offering Emily his arm. "Shall we?"

She accepted his escort, which kept her weak knees from buckling, and allowed him to guide her inside Seaton Hall's medieval foyer. Tapestries hung on the walls, adding color to the otherwise grey granite stones. Emily's heart ached at the sight of the flowers placed on display, precisely as her grandmother liked them.

"How is she?" Emily asked her grandfather when she and Stratton met him in the parlor.

"Much like yesterday," Grandpapa said, his voice hoarse. "No signs of improvement."

"I'm so sorry." Emily stepped forward and wound her arms around him in an affectionate hug. Releasing him, she said, "I was hoping I might be able to see her again."

Grandpapa tilted his head. He glanced at Stratton with an assessing look that brooked no nonsense. "You've every right to, Emily, but why on earth would you bring the Duke of Stratton with you?"

Emily blinked. She'd believed her grandmother might have mentioned their conversation, but it seemed this wasn't the case.

She raised her chin. "The duke and I have been secretly courting these past two weeks. Mama and Papa don't even know, but it's the reason I turned away Millfield. I wasn't planning to say anything yet, but in light of what's happened, I'd like to share the news with Grandmama. It will please her to know that I'll soon be settled."

Grandpapa frowned. "I agree, but I don't understand the secrecy, Emily. Stratton's an excellent match, unless there's a reason your parents do not approve?"

"Oh no." She waved a hand while trying to think of an explanation. "It's not that. It's just…um…"

"Lady Emily and I have had our differences in the past and have only recently become reacquainted," Stratton said, stepping forward. He placed his arm around Emily's shoulders and drew her close to his side. When he spoke next, the warmth in his voice turned her legs to mush. "We wanted to get to know each other properly without the attention and fuss we'd face if our courtship were publicly known."

"This may surprise you," Grandpapa said after a brief hesitation, "but I rather approve of that notion. It's important to know who you're planning to spend your life with. Figuring that out is far more easily done when you're not under scrutiny."

"Our thought exactly." Stratton spoke so convincingly Emily almost believed they truly were courting.

It's just pretend. You mustn't forget that.

"So you'll keep this a secret until we're ready to

make a public announcement?" she asked even as her heart gave a few extra beats.

"Of course." Grandpapa's eyebrow's dipped. "Your grandmother's maid was tending to her when you arrived. I'll go and see if she's finished so you can be shown up."

He departed, leaving Emily alone with Stratton and Georgina, who remained some distance away, near the door. Emily glanced around, feigning interest in the room despite being very familiar with the space. She was keenly aware of Stratton's proximity. One small step to the right and she'd bump into him.

It was strange how bold she'd felt in his presence while in the carriage. Now that they were more or less alone – or at least out of anyone's earshot if they chose to whisper – their flirtation, if that was what one might call it, made Emily feel awkward.

She supposed the incident needed addressing, only doing so would be acknowledging that she might possibly harbor some deeper feelings for Stratton. The whole situation was made worse by the fact that she was the one who'd placed her ankle against his boot. He'd simply stretched out his legs.

Should she apologize?

No, she did not dare.

Instead she said, "The explanation you gave Grandpapa was very inspired. Thank you."

"It wasn't much different than the truth."

She glanced at him then and saw that he was studying her with sharp interest. A shiver slid down her spine. She quickly averted her gaze and went to admire the porcelain figures that stood on the fireplace mantle. They'd been gifted to Grandmama by her parents when she was a child.

"She's ready to see you," Grandpapa said, returning a few moments later.

Emily turned and saw that Stratton offered his arm. She crossed the floor to where he stood, ever conscious of the heat flooding her cheeks. Unable to look him directly in the eye, she kept her gaze firmly upon the door as she linked her arm with his. Together, they followed Grandpapa from the room and climbed the stairs in the foyer.

They'd almost reached the upstairs landing when Stratton slowed his pace, holding Emily back. He dipped his head and when he spoke next, the low rumble of his voice had the most delightful effect on her nerves.

"Regarding what happened between us in the carriage..."

He wished to speak of this now?

Emily shot him a hasty look. "Nothing happened."

"I disagree."

"Our legs touched, that's all." She'd returned her attention to Grandpapa, who'd stopped to wait for them outside Grandmama's bedchamber door.

"Yes," Stratton agreed, "but it was the way in which they touched that demands addressing.'

She knew he had a point, but she really had no wish to discuss it. Certainly not now. "It will have to wait until later."

"Just tell me it meant something to you."

How could she possibly find the courage to do so when it felt as though her world was ending?

Impossible. Stratton demanded too much.

She shook her head. "I think you're making too much of this."

He stiffened slightly beneath her touch. "Of course. How foolish of me."

She wished she were able to say something more but they'd reached Grandpapa now, denying her the chance.

If only Stratton had waited for a more suitable time to broach the subject. Now she was left feeling like she'd betrayed him somehow.

Emily huffed a breath and followed her grandfather into the bedchamber where her grandmother lay. The curtains had been drawn to let light in and a window stood open to allow for fresh air to enter the space. Swallowing hard, Emily let go of Stratton's arm and approached the bed.

It was in many ways harder today than it had been the day before. Time had passed in the meantime, bringing her grandmother closer to death. Emily's throat tightened and her eyes began to sting when she saw the difference twelve hours had made. Her grandmother seemed a lot wearier now, as though she found life too exhausting and longed for a rest.

Emily took her hand and lowered herself to the edge of the bed. "I've returned, and I've brought the Duke of Stratton with me. Grandmama, I'd like for you to meet my suitor."

Her words were so raspy, Emily wondered if her grandmother could understand what she said. A handkerchief materialized before Emily's eyes and when she glanced up, she saw that it was Stratton who'd come to her aid. What stunned her though, was that his eyes glistened as though he too were struggling to keep his emotions at bay.

"Thank you." Emily took the handkerchief from him and dabbed at her eyes.

Grandmama's pale blue eyes found the duke. "A... pleasure. Emily did say...but I didn't...believe her. You're not...you're not...didn't think you the marrying sort."

Stratton placed one hand on Emily's shoulder. When he spoke, his voice was so soft and tender it made Emily weep even harder. "I wasn't until I met your granddaughter. That is, she and I met many years ago, but our encounters with one another weren't the best. It took time, years in fact, before the chance to get to know each other properly presented itself. Having spent more time in her company these past two weeks, I've grown to appreciate how incredible Lady Emily is. In truth, she's the most remarkable woman of my acquaintance."

Emily struggled to breathe on the heels of this speech. Her heart was thumping madly against her breast. Goodness, the man played the part of smitten beau well. She almost worried she might be in danger of swooning.

"When…will you…marry?" Grandmama asked.

A startled laugh rose from Emily's throat. "Goodness gracious, Grandmama. We've only been courting a short while. I've yet to receive a proposal."

Her comment seemed to remove what little energy Grandmama had been able to put on display. "My…dearest…wish… See you married."

"And I shall be," Emily told her while tears streamed down her cheeks. "I promise."

Grandmama shifted her gaze to Stratton. "Can you…give the same…assurance?"

"Of course," Stratton said without hesitation. "Allow me to put you completely at ease, Lady Seaton."

Emily breathed a sigh of relief. She wasn't sure how she would ever thank him for what he was doing for her today. It was beyond kind. She caught his gaze in the hope of imparting her gratitude, and was stunned when he lowered himself to one knee before her.

"Oh my," Grandpapa murmured.

"What are you doing?" Emily asked. It seemed obvious, but she simply couldn't believe it. This wasn't part of the plan.

Stratton carefully took her free hand while holding her gaze. "I see no reason to wait any longer. Not when these past two weeks spent with you have given me so much joy. Your kindness is unmatched by any other, your companionship so delightful I cannot imagine living without it. I want you in my life, Emily. As my wife and duchess. If you will have me."

"I..." Emily stared at him, at the sincerity burning in his eyes. It was confounding and had the effect of making her mind go blank. All she knew in that instant was him. And yet, what he was asking was no small thing.

Get a hold of yourself.

It's all part of the act.

"This is the part...where you say, 'yes,'" Grandmama rasped.

Emily blinked while a thousand thoughts sped through her mind. She'd come here to make sure her grandmother died with the peace of knowing that one of her grandchildren would get married. It was never her intention to pretend she and Stratton were engaged. By getting down on bended knee, he was forcing her hand. How could she refuse without letting Grandmama down?

She had to say yes, there was no other choice.

"Yes," she told him while feeling as though she were watching herself in a tragic play. Not even the happiness bubbling inside her when Stratton responded with a broad smile, was real.

This had gotten completely out of control.

"Well get off the floor, man," Grandpapa said, "and kiss your fiancée."

Concern flickered behind Stratton's eyes for the very first time. He gave Emily a hesitant look before rising. The happiness bubbling inside her died. She'd been right. It was just for show and this proved it.

"I don't think that's very proper," Emily said in an effort to stop the situation from escalating further. Stratton clearly had no desire to kiss her and, while she could not say the same, she really didn't want to be kissing a man unless he wanted to kiss her as well.

"Nonsense," said Grandpapa. "You're engaged now, we're family, and you are not out in public. So go on. You ought to seal the deal."

"He's right," Stratton said. Without further warning, he pulled Emily into his arms and pressed his mouth to hers in a kiss so swift she scarcely had time to register what was happening before it was over.

Her legs wobbled and she reached out her hand, grabbing hold of Stratton's lapel while she fought to regain her balance.

"Well done," Grandpapa cheered. "Congratulations on your engagement. I can't wait to share the good news with your parents."

Emily froze. "You said you would keep it a secret."

"When you were just courting I saw no reason not to. Now that you're getting married, your grandmama and I will both want to celebrate with them."

Oh God. What had she done?

"I'm so…so…happy for you," Grandmama said between strained breaths. "Once you have children, you'll know what it means…to be truly blessed."

Emily stared at her. This could not be happening.

"Thank you," she managed, feeling as though every part of the orderly life she knew was coming apart at the seams. To say nothing of Stratton's life. He'd done this to help her and look where that had led him. She couldn't even look at him on account of how awful she felt. It didn't matter that he was the one who'd made matters worse. The only thing of importance was that he'd never have done so if she hadn't asked for his help.

At least Grandmama smiled. That was something, but was it enough to make up for this utter disaster? Somehow, she'd have to find a way to fix it, but now wasn't the time. The promise of loss was too crippling. She couldn't think, could barely find her next breath.

It felt like the air had been sucked from the room.

Yet somehow, she had to find the strength to hold it together, just long enough to get out of the house.

So she took a deep inhalation and spoke past the lump in her throat.

"It's been wonderful seeing you again, but we probably ought to get going." Leaning forward, she placed a kiss to her grandmother's cheek and told her softly, "I love you with all my heart, Grandmama."

"I love you too, Emily."

The words caused additional tears to fall as Emily took her leave. She wiped them away with Stratton's handkerchief while making her way to the carriage. Once inside, she focused on staring out the window as they drove away from Seaton Hall. She could not look at Stratton, even though she knew there was so much for them to address.

If only it would all go away by itself so they could return to normal.

CHAPTER TEN

Callum was not sure what to think or how to feel. He considered Lady Emily who gave every impression of not wanting to deal with the swift progression of their relationship this afternoon. By all accounts, they were engaged now. Once her parents found out, it would be real.

Did she hate him for choosing to ask for her hand?

He'd only done so when he'd realized how important it was to Lady Seaton. The words he'd spoken had come with ease. He'd not even had to think, he'd just said them. They'd been honest and heartfelt. It hadn't been hard. In truth, he'd imagined the proposal was real while he spoke. Not once had he thought of it as an act.

Not until after.

And then he'd kissed her.

He'd had to, he'd tell her if she demanded an explanation later. To be honest, he'd welcomed the excuse the situation had offered. His gaze dipped to her mouth and his stomach instantly tightened with the memory of the softness he'd found there. It had been brief. Too brief. But such was a kiss when it happened in front of family. Allowing himself to be swept away by passion would not have been very proper.

So he hoped he'd be given a chance to improve his effort later.

Would she be amenable to such an idea? Or would she push him away?

He longed to find out, but how? Getting her alone was impossible with her maid always at her side.

Callum sighed as he settled against the squabs. He wanted to talk to her about all that happened, to be reassured that it hadn't affected their friendship. Not an option. The subject was far too personal to let Georgina overhear.

Still, it had to be addressed. Not doing so would only make it more awkward.

He considered his choices which were few considering their current location in a closed carriage. It wasn't as though he could ask Lady Emily to take a turn of the room with him so they could speak with a bit more privacy.

"I'm hungry," he blurted, with precisely the sort

of clumsiness he'd always managed to put on display in Lady Emily's presence. He ignored it. "Let's stop at the next inn."

"London isn't far," Lady Emily said, still not looking at him. "Can you not wait to eat until you get home?"

"No."

She sighed as though he were proving to be a huge inconvenience. "All right."

Callum tapped on the roof to inform the driver, and they pulled to a halt shortly after. Lady Emily hadn't been wrong. London was already visible on the horizon. It wouldn't take more than twenty minutes at most for them to reach it, another fifteen before they arrived at his home.

Ignoring that fact, Callum opened the carriage door and climbed down. He helped Lady Emily and her maid alight, then led the way inside the inn where he quickly acquired a table in the far corner.

He pulled out a chair for Lady Emily so she could sit, then turned to Georgina. "I believe I forgot my pocket watch in the carriage. Can you please go and fetch it?"

"Of course, Your Grace."

Callum waited for her to walk away before claiming the seat directly beside Lady Emily. Dismissing her stiff posture, he leaned in and whispered. "We need to talk about what has happened. Ignoring it won't make it go away."

"I wish it would," she murmured. "A courtship, that was all this was meant to be. A faux arrangement we could both walk away from with ease by simply deciding that we don't suit."

"Don't we?" His poor heart ached from the sting of her words.

She shook her head. "We've only recently started to tolerate one another. To get engaged feels like leaping off a cliff with a blindfold on. It wasn't supposed to happen."

"I know, but it felt like the right thing to do in the moment." He took her hand and gave it a gentle squeeze. "I'm sorry if it was the wrong move to make."

"You've nothing to apologize for." Lady Emily sniffed. "I got you into this mess when I asked you for an unreasonable favor. It is I who ought to be sorry."

"You were only trying to make your grandmother happy. I understand that. In fact, the length you're willing to go for her only proves what a wonderful person you are."

"I don't feel wonderful at the moment."

He considered that with an increasing sense of sadness. "Would it truly be such a bad thing if you and I were to marry?"

"Stratton, you—"

"Please, call me Callum." When she looked like she might protest he told her, "We are by all accounts engaged. Will you permit me the honor of using your given name too, without the honorific?"

She hesitated briefly before eventually nodding. "I've been thinking of how to solve this conundrum. If we tell Mama and Papa the truth, they can help make it go away."

A serving woman arrived at that moment denying Callum the chance to comment. Georgina joined them in the next instant. She apologized for not finding the pocket watch Callum had known to be in his pocket, and his conversation with Emily effectively ended.

Callum frowned. There was so much more to be said. Unfortunately, it would now have to wait.

"We'll go to Rosemont house directly," Callum informed the driver when they returned to the carriage after their meal.

Emily sent him an odd look. "We're supposed to be dropping you off first."

"I'll return home after we finish our talk."

She frowned at him but didn't comment. Instead, she positioned herself on the bench with a sullen expression that made him chuckle. She truly was lovely, even when she looked like the world was against her.

When they arrived at Rosemont House, Emily led the way inside while Callum followed behind. He'd just finished handing his hat and gloves to the butler when Emily's mother entered the foyer.

She stared at the assembled group in surprise. "Larrow said you went back to Seaton House."

Emily pulled at the ribbon holding her bonnet in place. "I did."

"If only you'd said something sooner. Papa and I are heading there shortly. You might have joined us instead of going alone." Mama glanced at Callum. "It seems you chose to call at just the right time, Your Grace. I wonder why you didn't bring Peter along."

"Might I have a word with you and Papa?" Emily asked her mother.

"Of course, but we'll have to make it quick since he and I would like to return before dark. Besides, it's not polite to leave your guest waiting."

"The matter I wish to address relates to Stratton as well. He has not come to call upon me, Mama. He and I went to Seaton Hall together and have just now returned. Together."

"Oh." Lady Rosemont looked visibly perplexed by this piece of information. "I'll, um...just fetch your father."

Emily looked at Callum for the first time since they'd entered the house. "Forgive me, but confiding in them seems like the most sensible idea at this point. It will hopefully help us find a way out of this mess."

Callum caught her arm before she could turn away. He waited until her eyes met his, then lowered his voice and asked, "Do you want a way out?"

"Don't you?"

He honestly wasn't sure. When he'd thought of settling down in the past, the idea had always made him break out in a sweat. He'd worried about every possible aspect, from whether or not he'd get along with his wife, to questioning his ability to be as good a father as his own had been.

But when he'd proposed to Emily, he'd experienced a sense of calm. Of course he'd told himself it was all pretend, but at the back of his mind he'd known it might end up being more. There had been the chance he'd not be able to walk away from the attachment. And still, he'd not experienced the slightest hint of panic.

If anything, holding her hand while on bended knee and telling her why he wanted to spend his life with her, had felt incredibly right. He wasn't sure he *did* want to find a way out of this 'mess', as she called it. If anything, it troubled him slightly that she didn't seem to share this opinion. Instead, she was very intent on putting an end to their brief romance.

She gazed at him, an expectant look in her eyes.

How easy it would be for him to lie to her now, to take the cowardly way out and simply pretend he wasn't a little bit thrilled with the idea of having her for his wife. Just thinking of having her by his side for the rest of his life warmed his heart.

"I'm not sure," he said.

Emily's lips parted. She shook her head as if

baffled. "Are you saying you want a real engagement with me?"

Was that what he was saying? The more he thought on it, the more certain he became. She'd make a wonderful wife, assisting in his guardianship of Peter, keeping him company in the evenings while they reclined by the fire, going on outings, and simply adding a spark to his life.

He nodded while every piece of heartache he'd felt since the death of his father collided and transformed beneath the incredible glow of her presence. She mattered to him and the thought of possibly losing her now just because he feared she didn't share his affection, was enough for him to give a quick nod.

She drew back with a small gasp.

"Yes," he said, cementing the idea just to be sure there was no doubt about his intentions.

"But it was only meant to be pretend." Her eyes glistened. "I never meant to trap you."

"You haven't trapped me, Emily." He reached for her hands and held them firmly between his own. "I am here by my own free will, ready to find out where this adventure might take us. Will you join me?"

She looked as though she might be sick. There were so many emotions dancing across her face, it was hard to keep up. In the brief time they stood there, Callum saw pain, anxiety, uncertainty, and finally, when all of those faded, a hint of joy. He chose to hold on to that while willing her to take a chance, not only on him but on them.

Her jaw tightened and then she finally nodded. "Very well. Yes."

Elated, Callum swept her into his arms and swung her around until they both grinned. It was the second time he'd proposed in the space of three hours, and while it was briefer, it was no less indicative of how he felt about her.

"What's happening here?" a deep voice asked.

Callum stumbled and nearly sent his bride-to-be flying. She squealed as he made a quick turn, coming to rest against the newel post at the base of the stairs. He set her down with the utmost care before turning to face her father.

"Forgive me, Lord Rosemont." His wife, Callum saw, stood at his elbow. Both looked as though they'd just seen an elephant playing dress-up. Callum straightened his posture and clasped his hands behind his back. "Lady Rosemont, I do apologize."

"I'm surprised to find you still in the foyer," Lady Rosemont said when no one else spoke.

"My wife says you'd like a word with us." The earl frowned, but the look he sent Callum was full of interest. "Shall we remove ourselves to the parlor?"

"Please make sure some tea is brought up," Lady

Rosemont said while eyeing someone who stood behind Callum.

He turned and blinked a few times when he spotted the butler and Georgina, both of whom he'd completely forgotten. Neither servant showed any hint of dismay over him having spun their mistress about or nearly dropping her in the process.

"Of course," said the butler. "I'll see to it that it's promptly delivered."

"We'll have to make this quick," Lord Rosemont said once they were all seated in the parlor. "My wife and I are due for Seaton Hall. We'd like to make the trip there and back before it gets dark."

"Understood," Callum said. Impulsively, he took Emily's hand and gave it a squeeze. The gesture did not go unnoticed. Eyebrows were raised by both her parents. "Allow me to get straight to the point. I've asked your daughter to be my wife and she has accepted. Pending your approval, of course."

Lady Rosemont beamed and clapped her hands together. "That's marvelous news."

Lord Rosemont looked less impressed. "Is this what you want, Emily?"

"Yes." The word was whispered and lacked the enthusiasm Callum had hoped for.

Her father seemed to latch onto that. "I wasn't even aware you were courting."

There was no denying the censure behind that statement.

"The truth is, we weren't." Emily took a deep breath, sent Callum a please-don't-hate-me-for-this kind of look, and proceeded to tell her parents all that had happened.

"It was kind of you to pretend for your grandmama's sake," Mama said, "but your grandpapa will be hurt if he finds out he helped with your scheme. Had you simply left it at courtship, you might have gone your separate ways later. A proposal of marriage – one made before them, no less – is far more serious."

"Though not as impossible to escape as an undesirable marriage," the earl pointed out. He glanced at Callum. "Once you say your vows, you'll be bound to each other forever."

"I understand the ramifications completely, my lord," Callum told him.

"And yet you wish to proceed." The earl leaned forward. "Why?"

A maid arrived with the tea tray Lady Rosemont had ordered, offering Callum a brief reprieve from the challenging conversation. Cups and saucers were swiftly distributed, and the tea poured before the maid slipped from the room.

"Well?" the earl pressed, an expectant look on his face. "What reason do you have for wanting to marry my only child and why should I permit it?"

"Papa," said Emily, her voice a touch more affirmative than before. "Stratton was only trying to help."

"And now he wishes to make you his wife in earnest. I do not think an explanation is too much to ask for."

"Of course not, my lord." Callum met the earl's gaze. "I understand your concern."

"Do you?" Rosemont scoffed. "Because your sudden interest in Emily certainly strikes me as odd. I mean, you've attended the same balls as she these past six years, yet you've not been seen dancing with her or speaking with her since she made her debut."

"If you'll recall, my lord, that didn't go very well," Lady Rosemont murmured.

"Perhaps not, but a gentleman finds a way to put that behind him if the lady in question is worth it."

Callum stiffened. "Your daughter is without question the finest woman I know. That is why I wish to make her my wife."

"According to what she's just told us, you were the one who contacted her first. Correct?" When Callum nodded, the earl said, "You were also the one who decided to get down on bended knee, effectively changing the rules of the plan you'd devised."

Callum didn't like where this was going one bit. "If you're suggesting that engineered this engagement from the beginning, you're wrong."

"Am I?" The earl picked up his teacup and paused before taking a sip. "Tell me, Stratton. What's your financial situation like these days?"

CHAPTER ELEVEN

A chill descended upon Callum's shoulders. He stared into Rosemont's demanding eyes while uncomfortably aware of Emily's presence. She'd stilled in response to the question and seemed to hold her breath now while waiting to see how he would respond.

He wouldn't lie, but he did have a question of his own that needed asking.

"It sounds as though you believe I might be struggling. You're not wrong, but I'd like to know how you found out."

"It's difficult not to notice when a duke begins using hackneys in favor of his own carriage." Rosemont tilted his head while studying Callum. "That aside, you and your reprobate friends have all been selling off various items in recent weeks. A source tells me you've put the furniture at your country estate up for auction. Adding two and two together isn't hard when one can recall the foolish excess that governed your lives just one year ago."

Callum hung his head in defeat. He'd worried his situation would become public knowledge as soon as he'd started ridding himself of his belongings, but what other choice had there been? He'd had expenses and no income. It wasn't until he'd received his share of the advance on the book he and his friends had written that things had started looking up. If only a little. The funds had provided some peace of mind but that didn't mean he shouldn't be cautious. He'd learned a valuable lesson from his mistake and intended to take better care of his money from now on.

"You're right." He lifted his gaze while doing his best to ignore Emily's presence. How disappointed she must be in him. It didn't bear thinking about at the moment. Later, when they had a chance to speak privately, he would explain. "I spent more than I could afford and have had to face the consequences, but you're wrong if you think me a fortune hunter. My only interest in Lady Emily is in Lady Emily herself. I do not care about her dowry, my lord."

"I wish I could believe that."

Callum dipped his chin. "You're free to craft the marriage contract in such a way that I'll have no access to her fortune."

"I can assure you that already crossed my mind,"

Rosemont told him. "What I wish to know is what you will be bringing to this marriage, Your Grace. Besides a title, that is."

"Most people would think a title enough," Callum said, his muscles tensing in response to the thinly veiled suggestion that he had nothing to offer besides that.

"I am not most people," Rosemont informed him. "I don't subscribe to the idea of buying a title through marriage. As an earl, I'm also of the opinion that my daughter will do just fine without becoming the Duchess of Stratton. So if that's your only asset, I must say I'm quite unimpressed."

"Naturally, I'm also offering myself, Lord Rosemont. I'd like to think that I am worth more than a title. Having spent a decent amount of time with your daughter lately, I believe she and I will suit each other well. We get along and seem to enjoy each other's company tremendously. Beyond that, I'm incredibly fond of her."

Rosemont exchanged a look with his wife before glancing at his daughter. "What say you, Emily? I'm sure we can find a way out of this for you if you desire."

Callum froze. His heart started pounding. This entire debacle, from going to Seaton Hall, to pretending they were courting, to him going down on bended knee, had been a colossal mistake from start to finish. But, it had also made him certain of one thing: he wanted Emily for his wife. Desperately.

He turned to her for the first time since this conversation began and saw the stunned look on her face. Her eyes were wide, her lips slightly parted, as though she were lost and had no idea of the direction in which to turn.

Callum took her hand and willed her gaze to meet his. Once it did, he told her gently, "I will always be your friend, ready to offer support and guidance whenever you need it. I'll do what I can to ensure your happiness, and while it is true that I'm not as wealthy as one might expect, I'm no pauper either. Stratton House is a fine place to live and although I've had to be frugal lately, I'm not yet in debt."

Thankfully this was something he'd managed to stay out of by refusing to take loans.

Indecision swam in Emily's eyes. "I worry this isn't the only thing you've been hiding."

"I wasn't hiding anything. It simply wasn't relevant until this moment."

"When my father brought it up."

She had him there. Even though he'd intended to be transparent with her about his finances, it was impossible for him to prove it. She'd always think he'd attempted to trick her into marrying someone who couldn't afford to keep his own carriage. Especially now that her father had questioned if he'd been after her money all along.

"Your grandparents will understand your reason for breaking off the engagement as soon as we tell them the duke tried to trap you," Rosemont said.

The insult stabbed at Callum's pride. Anger burn at the base of his skull. He fisted his hands and sent the earl a disdainful glare. "I did no such thing, my lord!"

"The evidence says otherwise." Rosemont huffed a breath and scrubbed his jaw. "Thankfully, no public announcement has yet been made."

"And I trust there have been no compromising acts in public," Lady Rosemont said.

"Of course not," Emily promised her mother.

"In other words," Rosemont said, "the engagement can be easily undone."

The earl's words clawed at Callum's heart. This couldn't be happening. Although it was true that he'd had no aspirations of marriage that morning, he was suddenly eager to cling to them with dear life.

For the briefest moment, when Emily had agreed to become his wife, joy had consumed him. He could not allow her father to ruin that – to turn her against him and crush the chance they had of a happily ever after. He had to stand his ground.

Praying she would believe him, he told her in earnest, "I would have told you about my financial problems eventually."

"When?" she asked, her voice filled with doubt and disappointment.

"I don't know, but I would have." He shook his head. "I'm sorry I didn't say anything sooner, but the chance to do so did not present itself, Emily. It wasn't the sort of thing I could bring up while I proposed in front of your grandparents, nor was it something I wished to discuss in front of your servants. You and I have not had a moment alone."

"That's true," she agreed. "Bu—"

"Had he wished to," Rosemont said, cutting her off, "he could have drawn you aside and told you about it discreetly. Without anyone else overhearing."

"Thank you." Lady Rosemont placed her hand on her husband's arm. "I do believe your point has been firmly made."

"I'm merely trying to protect our daughter," the earl grumbled.

"I know, Papa. You've always looked out for me and I'm grateful for that." Emily turned to Callum. "Do you swear to me upon your honor that you've not tried to deceive me?"

"Of course."

She held his gaze. "To be honest, I believe there's more to marriage than the wealth provided by each party. At least I'd like there to be."

"Me too." He took her hand and held it firmly within his own. "As I mentioned before, I want to marry you, not your dowry. The contract can reflect that."

"Did you also mean what you said about being fond of me?" This question was spoken in barely a whisper.

He squeezed her hand. "Yes. Having gotten to know you, I've realized there is no other woman I'd rather wake up next to each morning, no other I'd rather spend my days talking to, and no other I'd rather kiss good night every evening. I want you in my life, Emily. Forever."

A slow smile pulled at her lips. "I feel the same way about you."

It wasn't a declaration of love on either one's part, but it was enough to make Callum's heart race with increased excitement. "Does that mean you'll still agree to marry me?"

She nodded. "Yes."

He could have leapt with joy, but since Lord Rosemont did not look like he'd approve of such a display in his parlor, Callum refrained. Instead, he schooled his features and asked his future parents-in-law, "Do we have your blessing?"

Rosemont looked like he might say no. He tightened his jaw, expelled a deep breath, and finally nodded. "If it is what Emily wants."

Relief swept through Callum. She would be his! He could scarcely believe his good fortune. He also couldn't wait to tell Peter. The boy would be thrilled to have Heidi come live with them.

Aware that the Rosemonts wished to be on their way, Callum stood, as did everyone else. "Thank you for your time. I'll not delay you any longer."

"I trust you'll make sure an announcement appears in the paper," Lord Rosemont said.

"Of course." Callum hesitated briefly before deciding to reach for Emily's hand. He raised it to his lips and pressed a kiss to her knuckles while taking an uncommon amount of pleasure in seeing her blush. "Until we meet again."

He'd wanted to make plans to see her the following day, but decided she might need a moment in which to adjust to the new course her life had taken. It was all so sudden, he felt rather dizzy himself. But, he reflected when he arrived home, he was also extremely happy. And since he longed to share his news with someone, he went in search of Peter as soon as he'd handed his hat and gloves to his butler.

"That's brilliant news!" Peter exclaimed. He was just as excited as Callum expected him to be. "I'll be able to take Heidi out for a walk every day. We'll play together all the time. Do you think she'll be able to sleep in my room?"

Callum grinned. "I've no idea. We'll have to ask Emily about that."

This didn't seem to dimmish Peter's joy. He actually laughed, which was something Callum found rather delightful.

Dawson appeared in the doorway. “Begging your pardon, Your Grace, but the Dukes of Westcliffe and Corwin are here to see you. Shall I show them in?”

Anthony and Brody had both come to call? Their timing couldn’t be better.

“Please let them know I’ll join them shortly.” He turned to Peter. “Will you excuse me for a bit? I need to speak with my friends but maybe you and I can play a game of marbles afterward?”

He tried to engage the boy in various games he’d purchased for him, but Peter’s constant response had been disinterest.

“I’ll set it up while I wait,” Peter said, surprising Callum in the best way possible

Impulsively, Callum reached out and pulled Peter into his arms so he could give him a tight hug. When he set him back on his feet, he ruffled his hair and gave him a sly smile. “Maybe you can be my best man at the wedding.”

Peter’s eyes grew to the size of saucers. “Really?”

Callum grinned. “I can think of no one more perfect for the part.”

He left Peter gaping and went to greet his friends who’d both been shown into the parlor. “You’ve no idea how glad I am to see you right now. I’ve got news that I’m terribly eager to share.”

“How intriguing,” Anthony said, his expression

curious. Standing next to the sideboard, he was in the process of pouring himself and Brody a drink. "Brandy?"

"Thank you." Callum grabbed the already filled glasses and brought them to the table. He set one down in front of Brody, who reclined on the sofa, and lowered himself to one of the armchairs. Keeping the wide grin that threatened at bay was a struggle. Eventually he had no choice but to let it win over. He raised his glass as Anthony came to join them. "I'm to be married, my friends."

Anthony lost his footing and spilled his brandy while in the process of claiming his seat. Brody choked on his drink.

"What?" both men asked at the same exact time.

Callum smirked and raised his glass in salute. He took a sip and savored the heat the brandy produced as it slid down his throat. "I proposed to Lady Emily today and she has accepted."

Anthony shook his head as though baffled, then raised his glass. "Congratulations, my friend."

"That's marvelous news," Brody said. "A bit surprising since I'd no idea you had an interest there, but I'm happy for you."

"Our wives will be pleased as well since Emily is a good friend to them both," Anthony said. "Have you considered a date?"

"Not yet." Callum still couldn't quite believe this was happening. It felt like a dream. "The plan so far is to make the announcement in the paper. Beyond that, it's all rather new."

"Well cheers to you and your fiancée," Brody said while extending his glass.

Callum clinked his own against it and drank. "Thank you. I look forward to celebrating a bit more with you both in the coming weeks."

"I trust you've told her about the book we're releasing?" Anthony asked.

"Not yet," Callum confessed. "I barely had the chance to address my poor financial state, which was brought up by her father."

"How does *he* know you're struggling?" Brody asked.

"Apparently people take note when dukes start parting ways with their belongings or when they stop using their own carriage in favor of hiring hackneys."

"Ah." Anthony grimaced. "I'd not really thought of that. Or at least, I'd not imagined anyone would be quite so astute."

"Rosemont probably took an increased interest in me when I began spending time with his daughter." Callum relaxed against his chair and stretched out his legs. "Whatever the case, the fact remains that Emily and I are betrothed."

"You yourself look like you can scarcely believe it," Brody said.

Callum sent him a sideways glance. "If I told you

about my history with Emily and how our engagement came to be, you'd have a hard time believing it too."

"Fill us in and we'll put that theory to the test," Anthony told him.

"Very well." Callum set his glass aside and proceeded to give his friends an account of the mishaps that had taken place between himself and Emily. He went on to explain how the two had put their differences aside in favor of helping Peter. Finally, he told them about the favor Emily had asked of him and how he'd decided to follow his instinct.

"You're right," Brody said once Callum had finished. "That is an unbelievable story."

Anthony frowned. "Elements of it are very familiar though, wouldn't you say, Brody?"

"What are you talking about?" Callum asked. "I've never told either of you about any of this before."

"True," Anthony drawled. He glanced at Brody while tapping his thumb against the side of his glass. "Brody?"

Brody, Callum had noted, had gone slightly pale. He stared at Callum. "You haven't mentioned the book we've written to Emily."

"That's what I said." He couldn't figure out why they both looked slightly horrified all of a sudden.

"It would probably be wise of you to do so," Anthony murmured. "Immediately, if not sooner."

"And I will. I just don't see the rush." Callum glanced at each of his friends in turn. "My having written a book is not a terrible thing, even if it is a romance. It's hardly going to have a negative impact on our marriage. If anything, it will improve upon it by securing an income. Besides, when I told Emily I like to write as a hobby she showed a keen interest. She even asked if I'd thought about publishing. Surely that means she'd be supportive."

"Callum." Brody shifted his weight on the sofa and leaned forward, his forearms resting upon his thighs as he met Callum's gaze directly. "You wrote the middle of the story."

"I am aware," Callum said with a scowl. "What of it?"

"Have you completely forgotten how you wrote one of the hero's friends?"

Callum opened his mouth, then promptly shut it again. A queasy sensation took root in his stomach. He gripped the armrest and swallowed. "Like a lovesick fool whose nerves kept getting the best of him whenever he met Miss Emelia Parker."

"And Emelia?" Anthony quietly asked.

It was getting increasingly hard to breathe. Callum tugged at this cravat. Hell, even the name he'd used was strikingly close to Emily. How could he have dismissed that?

He forced himself to answer the question. "Like

an unforgiving shrew who doesn't deserve Mr. Dalton's affection."

"If I recall, they were described as always stumbling into each other," Brody said, his expression grim. "Much like you've just described yourself stumbling into Lady Emily numerous times. It does make one wonder."

"The incidents are only mentioned in passing. They play no larger role in the plot." There was no reason for anyone to draw a parallel, Callum decided, attempting to relax. "It's hardly noteworthy."

"Are you certain Emily will share that view?" Anthony asked.

"She may not even read the book," Callum said. He was suddenly bothered by the unnecessary amount of worry his friends were causing.

Brody gazed at him in dismay. "Of course she will when you tell her you wrote it."

This was probably true. "I'll simply have to not tell her then. The author will be anonymous anyway."

"I don't recommend that you start your marriage with a lie," Brody said. "If I were you, I'd get ahead of the problem by speaking with her straight away. Tell her about the book and what she'll find when she reads it. Explain that you wrote it before you fell madly in love with her."

"I'm not really ready to use that word yet," Callum hedged.

"Doesn't matter," Brody insisted. "The only thing that counts is the fact that she'll be less hurt if you open your heart completely."

Anthony, who'd fallen quiet for a few minutes suddenly added, "It may already be too late."

Callum froze. "What do you mean?"

"Brody and I came to give you some news of our own. The Lady Librarian has informed Ada that she has begun reading our novel and that she expects to have finished it by the end of the week."

"That's excellent news," Callum said. "I don't see how it relates to the problem of Emily possibly reading the book though."

Anthony's jaw tightened. "I'm not supposed to know this, so it is imperative that you keep what I am about to share with you both a secret. Do I have your words of honor?"

"Of course," Callum and Brody assured him in unison.

"Very well." Anthony took a deep breath and expelled it. "Emily *is* The Lady Librarian."

Callum gaped at his friend. It felt like a ton of bricks had been launched directly at his sternum. He blinked. "I beg your pardon?"

"I'd no idea," Brody muttered, "although it does make a great deal of sense."

"How?" Callum demanded. "How does Emily

being the most influential book reviewer in London make even the tiniest bit of sense?"

Brody sent a swift glance in Anthony's direction and shrugged. "From what I gather, she's extremely fond of reading."

"Many people are," Callum said. He shoved his fingers through his hair and stood. "That doesn't make them famous reviewers."

"I suppose not," Brody agreed while Callum began to pace. He had to think this through and then he had to figure out what to do. The more he delved into the situation, the greater his concern. Anthony and Brody were right. If Emily read the book, as she was apparently already doing, she was bound to suspect his involvement.

Leaving his friends in the parlor, he hurried to the library and collected the book from the shelf where he'd placed it. He flipped through the pages, searching for the part that threatened to ruin everything he'd just gained.

The segment wasn't long, but it was enough.

Sutherland glanced at Mr. Dalton, who appeared rather tense this evening. Having recently entered the packed assembly room together, they'd positioned themselves to the right of the entrance. From there, they had an excellent view of the dance floor, it being slightly lower than where they stood.

"Are you well?" Sutherland asked of his friend while

attempting to catch a glimpse of the woman who'd captured his heart. She was supposed to be here.

"As well as I can be with Miss Emilia Parker present." Mr. Dalton sent Sutherland a sidelong glance. "I swear, I'm forever making the wrong move when she is near."

"How so?"

Mr. Dalton snorted. "I've stepped on her toes, toppled her into a fountain, spilled punch down the front of her gown, tripped her up, and caused her to catch on fire. I'm not myself around her."

Sutherland raised an eyebrow. "Sounds like you might be smitten."

"Highly unlikely," Mr. Dalton grumbled.

"Oh? And why is that?"

"Because I would have to like the lady in question for that to be true. But how can I do so when all she ever does is curse me for being clumsy? No, indeed, Miss Emelia Parker is, without doubt, the very last woman upon this earth for whom I would ever develop a tendre. Frankly, if she treats other gentlemen as she treats me, it's no wonder she's not yet married."

Callum stared at the page while panic stormed through him.

Bloody hell, he was in trouble.

CHAPTER TWELVE

It was difficult for Emily to come to grips with every emotional up and down she'd experienced since she'd risen that morning. So much had happened. She'd gone to Seaton Hall with Stratton – Callum as he'd insisted she call him – feigned a courtship, which had turned into a proposal, and ended up properly engaged.

Had she known this was how her day would proceed, she would have imagined it making her unbelievably anxious. Instead, she felt surprisingly calm. Somehow, with every word he'd spoken in favor of marriage – even when they had both been pretending – had assured her. He'd made her believe this could work.

It was most unexpected. Two weeks ago she would have denied the possibility of becoming his wife. How easily life could change in what felt like the blink of an eye.

Beaming with pleasure, she settled into her favorite chair and opened the book she'd started the previous day. A romance novel was just the thing at the moment, now that she too was falling in love.

She giggled at that thought while her heart beat with endless pleasure.

It was silly perhaps, but Callum's proposal, and what he'd said since then, had swept her off her feet. Yes, he'd failed to reveal the state of his finances, but he'd assured her he would have done so once given the chance. And she'd believed him. He was a wonderful man who'd even gone so far as to tell her parents that he was fond of her.

A giddy sensation overcame her. She bit her lip and wondered when Callum might call upon her again. Tomorrow, she hoped. She really could not wait to see him or to try and steal another kiss. The one they'd shared in front of her grandparents had been too quick.

With a chastising shake of her head, she forced herself to focus on the text before her. It was easy to sit and daydream about her handsome husband-to-be, but that would not get her closer to writing the review she'd promised Ada.

Doing so would not be a struggle. Emily had been correct in trusting her friend. The style was fresh, the plot intriguing. She still couldn't figure out how an inn-keepers daughter might marry an earl and hoped there would be a really good explanation for it.

She bowed her head, read a few pages, and chuckled. Sutherland possessed the most wonderful sense of humor. When he'd spoken to his friend, Mr. Dalton, just now, it almost reminded her of something Callum might say.

And now she was comparing Callum to a fictional character.

She rolled her eyes and kept reading, only to frown a few pages later when Mr. Dalton mentioned his wish to avoid Miss Emelia Parker. Emily read the next line, and the next, with increasing concern. Her heart, which had been dancing about just an hour ago, was now limping along.

The incidents Mr. Dalton had referred to were not just similar to the ones she'd experienced with Callum. They were identical. Each had been mentioned, which made it impossible for her to think it coincidental.

A stabbing sensation pierced her heart. Callum must have spoken to Ada for this to have been included in the story. He was Westcliffe's friend, but Ada was Emily's friend, and Emily could not imagine Ada doing something so hurtful.

Unless…

Emily stilled as she thought back on her conversation with Ada a few weeks prior. Ada had asked if she would review a book. Not once had she said it was she or Anthony who'd penned it. Emily had made that assumption entirely on her own.

She leafed back a few pages and read from there. The style was horribly familiar. She'd not been wrong when she'd imagined Sutherland's voice belonging to Callum. His personality shone through in every aspect of the writing. There was no doubt in her mind. *He'd* written this.

It suddenly made sense. He'd told her he enjoyed writing, but he'd also told her he'd never been published. Emily gritted her teeth while fighting the urge to scream. Yet another thing he'd lied about.

She tossed the book aside, not caring that it landed on the floor with a thud.

Her mind raced. She had to break off the engagement. Which meant that everything she'd done to make her grandmother happy would go to waste. But how could she marry a man who'd used her as inspiration for one of the most dislikeable characters in his book?

The unhappiness she felt in the moment was crushing. Her dear grandmama was dying and just when she thought she'd found the strength to get through it, Callum revealed himself to be hateful and vindictive.

Well, she could be vindictive too.

She crossed to her desk and had just taken her seat when someone knocked on the door.

"Yes?"

Larrow entered. "The Duke of Stratton is here to see you, my lady."

Emily gulped down a breath as the pain in her breast intensified. She would have welcomed his visit an hour ago. For a second she wondered why he'd returned so soon after his departure, only to realize she did not care.

"You may tell him I'm not at home."

"Of course, my lady."

Emily waited until she was once again alone before retrieving a crisp piece of foolscap from her desk drawer. She dipped her quill in the inkwell and started to write.

Seductive Scandal

A critical review.

Despite being passably enjoyable at times, it was impossible for me to finish this novel. The author has crafted a fantasy where an innkeeper's daughter marries an earl. While this might have been an amusing tale if tackled correctly, the plot became too ridiculous and the characters too inconsistent for it to provide an enjoyable read. It is not a commendable story but rather one that may help pass the time if one is truly pressed for some entertainment.

I give it one cup filled with lukewarm tea.

Emily set her quill aside and blotted the page. Once this had been accomplished, she folded it, sealed it, and addressed it to her editor. Georgina, who often saw to such matters, would deliver it to *The Mayfair Chronicle* in the morning if Emily asked it of her. Which she wouldn't. To do so would be hateful and wrong.

She stared at the sealed review for a moment. It had only made her feel marginally better while she was writing. Now that she'd finished, she just felt more wretched. Which wasn't fair at all. This was Callum's fault. He was the awful person who'd gone and betrayed what she'd thought they had. But it was a lie. She'd been tricked into falling for someone whose dislike of her was so extensive he'd chosen to put it in writing.

How could she have been so stupid?

Papa had been right, but she'd been too blind and too eager to think the best of Callum to see what was suddenly so very clear. *He'd* contacted *her*. *He'd* made sure they spent time together. *He'd* been the first to show hints of affection and *he* was the one who'd used the pretend courtship to his advantage. He'd proposed in front of her dying grandmother, leaving her with no other choice than to accept.

He'd cunningly forced her hand while making it look like he actually cared about her.

What sort of twisted person did that?

And he wasn't done yet. Emily was certain of it. He'd dismissed her dowry, so money wasn't his end goal. She shook her head. The only thing she couldn't work out was his motivation. If he truly disliked her as much as his writing suggested, why shackle himself to her for the rest of his life?

Unless he was even more diabolical than she imagined.

A woman became a man's property once they married. He could sell her off if he chose to do so, or simply humiliate her until she feared leaving the house. In short, he could make her life hell once he put a ring on her finger.

Emily trembled at the idea. The Callum she knew would not be so cruel. Then again, she had to accept that she did not know him at all. For even if his opinion of her had changed in recent weeks, he'd made no mention of the book he'd written. He had, in short, kept it a secret.

And not the good kind of secret that ended with cake, flowers, and happiness, but rather the unforgiveable kind intended to see her destroyed. Why else would he have written it? What possible motivation could he have had if not to immortalize her as an unkind shrew who didn't deserve to be loved?

She heaved a big breath and nearly choked on the air when she tried to expel it. Oh, how she loathed him. He'd used an innocent boy to lure her, for heaven's sake. It was beyond sinister.

The sound of the front door opening and closing caught her attention a good hour later.

Emily stood and went to greet her parents. She met them in the foyer.

"I think I've made a terrible error in judgement."

Mama and Papa shared a look before ushering her toward the parlor with Mama quickly assuring Larrow that they would be ready for supper soon.

"What's happened?" Papa asked as soon as he'd shut the door. "Has this got something to do with Stratton?"

She nodded. "I cannot marry him."

"But..." Mama shook her head as she lowered herself to the sofa. "Word of your engagement is already spreading."

"How is that possible?" Emily couldn't imagine her mother was right. She and Papa had gone straight to Seaton Hall and back. Whom would they have spoken to?

"Since you and Stratton were in agreement, we saw no reason to whisper about it while we were at Seaton Hall." Papa, who wore a severe expression, clasped his hands behind his back. "Your grand-mama was extremely pleased on your behalf, by the way. Despite her weakened state, she wouldn't stop talking about your impending nuptials. Servants will have heard. Your aunts, uncles, and cousins too."

Emily lowered herself very slowly to one of the armchairs. "They were all there?"

"They arrived this afternoon, in response to the letter I sent them."

"Of course they did." Emily sighed.

"We've assured them you would invite them to your wedding," Mama murmured.

Emily glanced at her mother and nodded. "Right."

Her entire body felt numb, her brain too.

It was too late. She was stuck. If her aunts knew, the whole world would soon be informed. Ending such an engagement would lead to scandal – a scandal that would affect her and her family, most notably her younger cousins.

"Will you tell us what has prompted this change of mind?" Papa asked. "You looked quite smitten with Stratton this afternoon. What's changed?"

"As it turns out, he's not who I thought him to be."

Papa held her gaze. "I'll assume that you're not referring to him being a duke without a fortune."

"He's written a book," Emily said while doing her best to keep her composure when all she wanted to do was cry. "I recognized one of the characters in it as me, and I was not depicted in a favorable light."

Papa straightened. "He insulted you?"

"Indirectly, yes."

"That bloody, good-for-nothing, scoundrel," Papa seethed. "I ought to call him out for this. That would certainly solve your problem. You cannot marry him if he's dead."

"Good heavens." Mama sent Papa a chastising glance. "Must you be so macabre?"

"When the situation calls for it," Papa grumbled. "Besides, you can't deny that I do have a point."

Mama puffed a breath and turned to Emily. "Has this book been published?"

"Not yet. It's set for release on Monday."

"So then he must have written it long before the two of you started your courtship. Am I right?"

"Yes, but that doesn't change the fact that he wrote it or that he chose not to tell me about it." Emily fidgeted with her skirt. "Why would he keep something so important from me unless he meant for the publication to come as a blow?"

"I know a man who can help us get to the bottom of this," Papa said. "Just give me the word and he'll pay Stratton a visit."

"I hope you're joking," Mama said while sending Papa a horrified look. He scowled and removed himself to the sideboard where he proceeded to pour himself a large drink. Mama gave her attention back to Emily. "Listen to me, dearest. A marriage is first and foremost built on trust and open communication. You cannot let yourself be influenced by suspicion and doubt. It's poisonous, Emily, and only serves to ruin what might be worth saving."

Emily crossed her arms. "He broke whatever trust we had by failing to communicate with me, Mama."

"I'm inclined to agree," Papa said before taking a sip of his drink.

Mama shook her head and sighed in frustration. "You're not being helpful, Lawrence. Must I remind you that you once thought the worst of me?"

Interest heightened Emily's alertness. Leaning forward, she met Mama's gaze. "How do you mean?"

Mama knit her brow and waved a dismissive hand. "He thought I was having an affair with one of his friends."

"What?" Emily turned to Papa. "When?"

"It was years ago," Papa admitted. "Shortly after we'd married. Turned out to be nothing more than my overactive imagination playing tricks on me."

"The point is, we talked," Mama said, "and by doing so we worked it all out. Your father realized I wasn't guilty and I forgave him."

"I'm not the only one guilty of making mistakes," Papa grumbled.

"Of course not," Mama agreed. "I've made plenty of my own. All I'm trying to say is that marriage, like any relationship, takes work. Deciding Stratton's at fault without letting him come to his own defense is unfair and unproductive. Unless there's something else at play and this is the excuse you needed in order to end things."

Emily flopped back against her seat. "He pretended to care about me, Mama."

"And who's to say he doesn't?" Mama raised her eyebrows. "People change their opinion all the time, but in order to do so, their experience needs to change too. It's possible spending additional time with you proved to Stratton that you're not the person he thought you to be. Based on the sincerity I heard in his voice earlier today, I'm inclined to believe that he truly fell for you, Emily. And if he deliberately kept what he'd written from you, then I believe this to be the real reason."

"Are you suggesting he lied out of love?"

Mama chuckled and sent Papa and knowing glance.

Papa held her gaze for a moment before eventually sighing. He turned to Emily. "How would you have reacted if you were in his position?"

Emily considered the question with care. During her six-year acquaintance with Callum, he'd vexed her to no end. She'd cursed him multiple times and had placed all blame for their calamitous run-ins with each other upon his shoulders.

However…

"I never would have written an ill word about him in the first place."

"But let's suppose you did. What would you do when you realized you were falling for someone you'd villainized? How would you feel?"

"I suppose I'd be embarrassed, possibly ashamed."

"And?" Mama pressed.

"Worried. I think I'd be terribly worried about them finding out since the last thing I'd want to do is hurt them." Emily straightened and stared at her parents. "But what if you're wrong? What if Stratton deliberately strove to hurt me?"

"Talk to him," Mama said. "It's the only way for you to get to the heart of the matter and find out the truth."

"And if he did indeed try to hurt you on purpose," Papa said, "I'll skewer him myself."

"Good Lord," Mama murmured while rolling her eyes.

Emily smiled for the first time that evening. Her parents had calmed her with their advice. They were right. Speaking to Callum and asking him to explain was the most reasonable option. And somewhere deep inside, beyond the hurt he'd caused her, she prayed he'd convince her they could be happy together. That, beyond all else, was what she longed for most of all.

CHAPTER THIRTEEN

Callum refused to be deterred. He *would* see Emily today, no matter how many times he had to call upon her. Hell, he'd camp on her front doorstep if need be. Talking to her was the only way forward.

Having her butler inform him that she wasn't in yesterday evening, had been like a slap to the face. He'd known she was there. He'd seen her bonnet and gloves on the foyer table behind the butler. Which meant she'd refused to see him.

Callum could only think of one reason why this might be. She had arrived at the part of *Seductive Scandal* he'd written.

He cursed himself for the millionth time for putting those references to their relationship in there. How stupid he'd been, yet at the time, he'd not really cared if Emily read it or not. Whether she took offense hadn't mattered back then.

Now was a very different story.

He wanted her in his life and for that to still happen, he'd have to apologize, explain, and grovel. Callum was prepared to do all three. He'd stopped by the hothouse to purchase a massive bouquet of flowers during his walk to Rosemont House. Anyone who saw him would know he was desperate.

Upon reaching his destination, Callum took a deep breath in an effort to slow his racing heart and calm his nerves. Never before had he been made to rely so completely on saying the right words. It was imperative he get it right when he saw her. Somehow, he had to make her believe in him. In them.

Deciding he'd never be ready to face what awaited beyond the Rosemont front door, he forced his feet forward and gave the knocker three solid raps. At just after two in the afternoon, he'd arrived within acceptable calling hours. Hopefully someone would be here and he would be granted entry.

Callum just hoped he wouldn't end up in the parlor with Emily's father.

The door was opened by the butler who gave him a very acerbic look. "Yes?"

"I've come to call on Lady Emily," Callum said while attempting to stop his bouquet from pushing against the butler. "Will you please let her know the Duke of Stratton is here?"

Of course the man knew who he was, but Callum

believed the mention of his formidable title might lend the kind of weight that would ensure he met with success.

He could not have been more wrong.

The butler didn't budge. "I regret to inform you that Lady Emily isn't at home."

"That's what you told me last night."

"And the same is true now, Your Grace. I'll be happy to relay a message on your behalf."

"Thank you, but I'd rather speak with her in person."

"In that case, I would suggest you return at a later date. If you'll excuse me."

The door started to close. Callum stepped forward and used his foot to block it. The butler raised a questioning brow, looking extremely critical of this complete lack of manners. Callum gave him a hard scowl.

"What about the Earl and Countess of Rosemont? Are either of them home? For if they are, I'd like to see them instead."

"No," said the butler. "They are not at home either. The entire family is out."

"Do you know when they are expected back?"

"I do not." The butler pushed at the door, squeezing Callum's foot. "Your Grace, I believe you're coming dangerously close to overstaying your welcome."

"Lady Emily is my betrothed," Callum told the

blasted gatekeeper. "I merely wish to know if she is well."

"I cannot say." The butler kept pushing.

"Oh, for the love of all that's holy," Callum shouted in a display that lacked all decorum. "I can't leave as long as my foot's stuck. You'll have to open the door."

The butler glared at him but eased the door open. Callum thrust the bouquet of flowers at him. "Please make sure these are placed in water and that Lady Emily receives them. I'll see you later when I call upon her again."

"No need to do so today," the butler said, his exasperation with Callum finally cracking his flawless veneer. "I don't know when she'll return, but it shan't be tonight. Good day, Your Grace."

The door slammed shut, though not before Callum was able to notice something important. It shocked him that he'd not seen it sooner, but he supposed the butler had hindered his view. Additionally, his purpose in coming had kept his attention upon his goal. But as the door closed and the butler stepped sideways, Callum had noted the black crepe adorning the foyer.

His mind raced. Lady Seaton must have died between yesterday and today, which certainly explained why none of the Rosemonts were at home. Still standing on the pavement in front of their house, he glanced around, unsure of what to do next.

He knew what he wanted to do, and that was to comfort the woman he loved.

Because yes, he did love her, didn't he? What point was there in denying it when every breath he took was with her in mind. Her grandmama was gone and if Callum was brave – if he truly wanted to prove his feelings for her trumped all else – he'd go to her and offer the reassurance she needed.

Intent on ignoring the fear of having her turn him away, Callum returned home at a near run.

He entered the foyer and tossed his gloves to his butler, calling to him as he started upstairs, "I need my horse saddled this instant."

"What's going on?" Peter asked. He'd arrived in Callum's bedchamber while Callum shoved clothes into a satchel.

"Lady Emily's grandmama…" Callum froze in the midst of the turmoil and stared at Peter. He'd been about to tell him the truth, but what if the news only served to remind him of his own loss? "Umm…"

"Did she die?" Peter asked.

Callum sagged against his dresser. "Yes. Unfortunately so."

Peter nodded. "Then you should probably go and give her a hug the way you did me. It'll make her feel less alone."

The comment speared Callum's heart. His eyes began stinging. Not once had he believed the affection he'd shown toward Peter when he'd arrived to collect him had made any impact. How wrong he'd been.

Callum crossed to where the boy stood and pulled him into his arms. "That's my intention."

He dropped a kiss on top of the boy's head and set him aside so he could finish his packing. He told him goodbye shortly after and went to collect his horse from the mews.

The journey to Seaton Hall didn't take long since he wasn't hampered by a carriage. He arrived there in under an hour.

"Your Grace," said the butler, recognizing Callum from his visit the previous day. "We weren't expecting you."

"I know, but when I heard what had happened I realized I needed to be here." He met the man's gaze and held it, relieved to find the look he received in return more welcoming than the Rosemont House butler's. "If it's no inconvenience, I'd like to convey my condolences to Lady Emily and her parents, as well as to the viscount."

"Of course. I'll see if they are accepting calls."

The butler left and Callum braced himself against the nearest wall. His hands were trembling. Knowing what was to come had his stomach twisted into all kinds of knots. He'd never been so damn nervous. Not even during that first fated dance with Emily.

This was worse. Much worse. One wrong word and he'd ruin everything.

Get a hold of yourself.

He straightened, squared his shoulders, and clasped his hands behind his back. Footsteps warned of the butler's return.

"I am to show you to the parlor," he said and gestured toward the room where Callum had met Viscount Seaton the previous day.

Callum entered the comfortable space. With no one else present, he crossed to the fireplace where several porcelain figures stood on display. He admired them all before going to look at the clock collection that sat on a nearby table.

"Grandpapa has always loved clockwork." Emily's hushed words prompted Callum to turn. "Grandmama gifted him most of those."

The defeated look on her face nearly slayed him. He went to her without caring if she was angry with him or if she might want to end their engagement. All that mattered right now was easing her suffering. The rest could wait until later.

So he pulled her into his arms and embraced her, hugging her close while she wept.

"Shh…" His hand swept up and down her spine in long soothing strokes. "You're not alone. I'm here. I'll always be here if you need me."

"It's so unfair," Emily cried. "She wasn't even that old."

"I know, sweetness, but she's with God now and at peace. Try to find strength in that."

A sob was all he heard in response to his words, so he simply held on and guided her through the worst of the storm until it faded. She gulped a few times, sniffed a little, and pressed her forehead against his chest while clutching at his lapels. A deep inhalation followed before she finally took a step back.

She swiped her eyes with the back of her hand, but the effort did little to stop the tears from flowing.

"What are you doing here?" Her voice was raw. "How did you know to come?"

"I guessed what had happened when I came to call upon you and saw your foyer decked in black crepe."

"Of course." Her attention went to the window and for a second it seemed like something had drawn her attention. Until Callum noted the faraway look in her eyes. It appeared she wasn't really present.

He wasn't surprised. She'd been dealt a terrible shock.

Reaching out, he caught her hand and she turned, her gaze dropping toward the spot where he held her. "There's a great deal I'd like to tell you, but right now I simply want you to know that I've come to offer whatever support you might need."

"I read what you wrote," she told him without raising her gaze. "I'm the Lady Librarian."

Callum's gut spun and a cold chill swept down his spine, but he fought his way past it. "I know. I realize I'm not supposed to, but I found out yesterday. That's why I called on you last evening, because I thought you might have read it, and I understand if it changes the way you feel about me."

"It made me doubt everything you and I have shared these past weeks, but your showing up here speaks volumes. I'm glad you came."

So was he. It would, he hoped, grant him the chance to make himself heard. He squeezed her hand.

"Will you be staying?" she asked, her gaze finally finding his.

He nodded. "As long as it takes."

"I'll speak with you later then." The words were barely more than a croak.

Callum drew her back into his arms and hugged her once more before letting her go.

It took a long time before she returned and when she did, she wasn't alone.

CHAPTER FOURTEEN

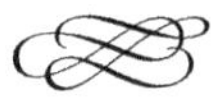

Emily felt both hollow and raw. It had been an extremely difficult day thus far. News of Grandmama's death had arrived at eight o'clock in the morning before she or her parents had gone down to breakfast. Arrangements had quickly been made, mostly by Papa, who'd immediately taken charge since Mama could do little but sit and weep.

Emily had done her best to console her, even though she herself had been gripped by loss.

The carriage ride had been a solemn journey. No one had spoken a word. When they'd arrived at Seaton Hall, Emily's aunts and uncles had all been ready to greet them. Silence had been the predominant theme, and it had been awful. It stood in stark contrast to Grandmama's spirited personality, making her loss all the more pronounced.

Now, surrounded by family in the Seaton Hall

parlor, Emily took the tea someone offered and drank, appreciating the soothing effect the heat offered.

How many tears had she cried?

She'd no idea, but it was a lot – a constant stream of agony that had dampened most of her handkerchiefs.

Her gaze wandered to where Callum sat, his expression as grave as the mood filling the parlor. His arrival had been a lovely surprise. Despite the pain he'd caused her, she'd needed him more than she'd realized. His embrace had been a wonderful comfort. And the fact that he'd chosen to be here also proved he cared. It lifted her spirits a little and gave her hope.

Perhaps Mama had been right. Maybe his feelings for her had changed since they'd started spending more time together. Would it then be fair of her to judge him for what his opinion of her had been before? Her own opinion of him had not been positive either.

No, but she wouldn't have put it in print?

She sighed and drank some more tea while her aunts and uncles spoke with her parents and Grandpapa in hushed tones. All had offered congratulations to her on her upcoming wedding, which had been a strange experience indeed since they were presently trying to plan for a funeral.

"Why must we sit here like this?" Emily blinked

at the realization that she had spoken the words out loud. She glanced around, aware the conversation had ceased and that everyone stared at her. "Forgive me. I'll just… I believe I'm in need of fresh air."

She stood while everyone tracked her movement.

"Shall I come with you?" Mama inquired.

"No. It's fine. I'll be fine."

The conversation resumed as she crossed to the door.

"We need to decide on the hymns," Aunt Marjorie, the eldest of the three sisters, said. "The vicar will want to know when he arrives."

"Andrew and I can go to Town and meet with the cabinet maker," Papa said. "If the service is going to take place tomorrow, we'll need a coffin."

"How about…"

Emily missed the rest of Uncle Andrew's words as she slipped from the room. It was a bright and sunny day outside, though perhaps a bit chilly, she reflected as she headed toward the rose garden. Maybe she should have collected her shawl. She stopped for a moment and considered returning to fetch it, except she really didn't wish to go back inside Seaton Hall right now.

What she needed was the liveliness to be found in the rustling of leaves and the twittering of birds. Grandmama had been an avid gardener. Her spirit was far more present out here than it was in there.

Hugging herself, Emily followed the graveled

path toward the roses. It had always been her favorite spot here, not only because of the perfect blooms or the lovely scent they produced in the summer, but because of the domed folly that stood just beyond it. Emily had always imagined it to be extremely romantic – the sort of place where a knight might find his maiden when he returned from the Crusades.

Her fingers trailed over a box-cut laurel hedge lining the path. She took a deep breath and inhaled the scent of autumn. Already, the leaves on the trees had turned bright shades of red, yellow, and orange. Soon the ground would be littered with them.

She smiled at the thought. When she was little, her grandparents would take her for walks as soon as there was a thick enough layer of leaves for them to stomp through. They'd all loved the crisp sound beneath their feet and the pretty display when they kicked the leaves up in the air.

The memory tightened Emily's throat. God, how she'd miss her grandmother.

Drawing to a halt, she stared at the rose bushes. All had been trimmed to the ground with not a single bloom left in sight. The bleakness of those thorny branches, devoid of colorful blooms, caused Emily's eyes to well with tears once again. She swiped them away with the back of her hand.

The sound of gravel crunching behind her made her to turn.

"I'm sorry to disturb you," Callum said, his expression grave. "I merely wanted to ask if you'd like some company."

She pressed her lips together and sniffed, attempting to collect herself. "Only if you're willing to cheer me up."

"There's nothing wrong with crying."

"I know, but Grandmama wasn't a dreary person. I think she'd prefer a lively tune played in her memory to the oppressing cloud of gloom everyone seems so determined to spread."

Hands in both pockets, he moved toward her slowly. "Very well. I'll do what I can to brighten the mood, although I'm not sure I'll be very successful. You see, there's a matter I cannot ignore. It must be addressed before you and I can move forward."

"I know." It was unfortunate, but he was correct. The book he'd written was like a huge boulder wedged between them. They had to acknowledge that it existed.

She resumed walking, keeping her pace slow until he fell into step beside her.

"You turned me away last night," he began.

It wasn't exactly a question, more of a factual statement, though it still demanded a response.

"Yes."

He sighed. "I can only assume this to be because of the book I helped write. There's a section in there that echoes the nature of our relationship prior to us becoming friends. I'm sorry for it, Emily. My intention was never to hurt you."

"I'm not sure I believe that. The incidents you describe in the book are identical to the ones you and I have shared in the past. Only, in the book, you come across as the poor mistreated victim while I'm a cruel shrew. It's not an accurate portrayal and contrary to what you've just said, it seems extremely vindictive."

"I'm sorry, but you're wrong. Emily, those characters aren't you and me. They're fictional. Miss Parker and Mr. Dalton were always intended to be at odds. Writing them was a challenge. I struggled to find a reason for them to be constantly clashing with one another, and that's when I thought I'd let myself be inspired by true events."

"Yet you chose to paint Mr. Dalton in a favorable light while making Miss Parker an awful person."

"Only because I was hurt."

She stopped at this and turned to face him. "How so?"

He glanced away, sending his gaze across the garden before speaking next. A slight twitch at the edge of his mouth and the way his throat worked as he swallowed, suggested he struggled to find the right words.

Eventually, he admitted, "I think I've had a bit of a tendre for you for a very long time. Since your debut."

"My debut? But that's six years ago."

"I know." He returned his attention to her and she saw the pained look in his eyes. "Remember when I told you how nervous you made me that evening?"

How could she forget? He'd shocked her with the confession. "You said you'd never seen a woman more dazzling."

He nodded. "As a result, I became a clumsy mess whenever I saw you."

"It always felt as though you were angry with me for getting in your way."

"You're not entirely wrong. I was angry with you, but not for getting in my way, Emily. I was angry with you for having such a crippling effect upon me. And for the way you reacted." He lowered his voice to a whisper. "You never gave me the chance to make amends."

"Only because you made me angry as well. You ruined more than one of my gowns and, given the fact that it kept happening, I believed you did it on purpose. As a result, I wanted nothing to do with you, Callum."

"And now?"

"You do not strike me as someone who's overly nervous." She narrowed her gaze. "Ever since asking me out for that walk in the park, you've been nothing but composed. It makes me question whether or not what you're saying is true."

He rocked back on his heels and turned his gaze sideways before he resumed walking at a moderate pace. Emily followed, keen on knowing if he would say more.

They followed a path that cut straight through the middle of the rose garden and led toward the folly. Callum removed his hands from his pockets and clasped them behind his back.

"Everything changed for me when we started interacting because of Peter," he told her. The comment was followed by a swift glance in her direction as if to ensure she'd heard him. "He gave me a purpose that forced my self-consciousness into the background. I finally managed to speak with you without feeling as though my brain was filled with wood filings and my mouth with wads of cotton. I was able to relax, especially through our exchange of letters, while getting to know you on a more personal level.

"This made it so much easier when I called on you at your home and later when we went for our walk. It gave the impression that we'd become friends, and that, in itself, removed a tremendous amount of pressure. I no longer viewed you as a goddess-like woman I constantly failed to impress. Your responses to my letters and the conversation we shared when I brought you the flowers, proved we not only had much in common but that we were certain to get along. It calmed me."

"I just wish you'd have told me about the book," Emily said. "Why didn't you?"

"There were numerous reasons." He frowned as he stepped onto the grass that led to the folly.

Emily sent a glance over her shoulder. They'd walked quite a distance from the house and if they kept going, they'd soon be out of view. She stopped, unsure of whether or not it was wise to follow.

He halted as well. "First of all, you should know that the man who wrote those words is not the same man who stands before you today. That said, the truth is I simply didn't think of it. The book was written before the summer. A lot has happened since then and besides, I didn't expect it to have the impact it's turned out to have."

"You didn't think I'd read it?"

A quick shake of his head informed her this wasn't the case. "I didn't give that any thought as I didn't know you were the book reviewer. But mainly, I didn't expect to form an attachment with you and for you to read it immediately after."

"This has nothing to do with our being engaged."

"Are you sure about that?"

She stared at him. "I would have been upset by it regardless."

"Probably, though not for the same reason as you are now."

"I don't follow."

"Because of what happens next in the book." He

gazed at her for a second and then his lips parted. "You didn't read past that scene, did you?"

"I must confess, I had no wish to."

He pinched the bridge of his nose and when he looked at her next, his eyes were filled with regret. Stepping toward her, he reached for her hand. His fingers were warm. The touch of them sent an electrical charge up her arm.

"The chapter breaks and we see Miss. Parker's perspective as she discusses Mr. Dalton with her sister."

"That makes no sense at all," Emily said. "Miss Parker isn't the heroine, nor does she have any relationship to her."

"It isn't written from her point of view," Callum explained, "but as an exchange Miss Partridge overhears. In it, Miss Parker has her own strong opinion of Mr. Dalton. The scene is intended to set up another romance that's meant to unfold in the next book."

"Are you saying Miss Parker and Mr. Dalton end up together?"

"Yes." His hand squeezed hers. "They actually fall madly in love. A bit sickening at times, I imagine, but that's all part of the fun."

"You're right. I would have been very upset if I'd read that last month."

"And now?"

She wasn't quite ready to tell him all was

forgiven. Not when something he'd said had led to additional questions. "You mentioned numerous reasons for choosing not to mention the book. What are the others?"

"First of all, a book is a very personal thing. It offers a glimpse of the author's mind, revealing private thoughts they'd never dare mention in public. Most importantly, however, is the fact that I'm not the only author, so speaking of it would have broken a promise I made to the others."

Emily blinked. "What do you mean you're not the only author?"

He gave her a funny look. "You still don't know?"

"What I know is that it would appear as though you have been keeping more than one secret from me."

His eyes widened. "Let us not speak of keeping secrets when you yourself are as guilty of that as I am."

The reprimand was a swift reminder of everything she herself had intended to share with him. When the time was right. "Who told you about me being the Lady Librarian?"

"Does it matter?"

"No. I don't suppose it does."

Silence fell between them, expanding until Callum blew out a breath and told her, "It was Westcliffe. He and Corwin are the other two authors."

Her lips parted for a brief second and then she

shook her head while allowing a broad smile to capture her lips. "Of course they are."

"You can't tell anyone."

"Your secret's safe with me," she promised. Her smiled faded and it became clear that her thoughts had strayed toward something else. She gave him a hesitant look. "Will you insist that I set down my quill if we marry?"

"If?"

"All things considered, I didn't want to presume."

He clenched his jaw. An intense emotion burned in his eyes. He sent a quick look over her shoulder, and then he suddenly spun on his heel and pulled her along behind him.

Emily gasped as she tripped, her hand grabbing hold of his upper arm in a desperate attempt to keep her balance. "What are you doing?"

"Proving something once and for all," he muttered.

Emily gasped as she quickened her steps, doing her best to keep up with his longer strides

"What's that?" she asked, a little alarmed by the wild determination with which he cut a path straight to the folly.

He didn't respond, nor did he slow his pace when they reached the domed marble structure. Instead, he led her inside the circular space and drew her toward the right, immediately behind a large pillar.

His chest rose and fell with each ragged breath as

he pushed her against the cool stone. He was close – too close for her to keep all her wits about her. Closer still, as he leaned in.

Emily's pulse leapt. Heat washed her face as he trailed his fingertips over the side of her face.

"Engaging in a fake courtship and getting engaged in the spur of the moment, have proven to me that I'm happiest knowing you will be mine. And no, I will not make you set down your quill once we're married – as we shall be if I have anything to say about it. Because if there's anything I have learned from spending these past few weeks together, it's that I love you."

Her heart fluttered. "You do?"

"Desperately, wholeheartedly, with every fiber of my being."

"I love you too," she confessed. "That's why it hurt as much as it did when I read what you'd written. It felt like you hated me in return."

"I could never hate you, Emily." His eyes, she saw, shone with emotion. "Please forgive me. I beg you. Give me the chance to prove myself worthy."

"Only if you forgive me for the secrets I kept."

He raised an eyebrow. "Secrets. As in more than one?"

"I don't just write reviews," Emily told him. "I also run a book club. We meet the first Saturday of every month."

"Is that all?" Callum asked, his piercing gaze holding hers.

He dipped his head as soon as she nodded, and crushed her mouth with his. This was not the paltry show of affection he had displayed when he had proposed. This kiss overwhelmed, it weakened her knees and forced her to cling to him in desperation. It was raw, completely improper, and utterly delicious.

The intimacy was extraordinary, the taste of him so divine she could not get enough. The need building inside her threatened to rid her of sensible thought. She was lost to sensation, and he was her guide.

"Exquisite," he murmured, the words whispering softly against her skin as he kissed a path over the edge of her jaw. One hand gripped her waist, the other sought out her thigh.

She shifted a little and arched up against him, hoping to offer whatever encouragement he required to further his exploration. He did not disappoint. His hand on her thigh tightened before sliding higher."

"Tell me to stop and I will," he promised.

"Not yet," she gasped as his teeth grazed her shoulder. "Kiss me again."

She didn't have to ask twice. His mouth returned to hers in a sensual exchange of forbidden yearning, each sweet caress alluding to something increasingly feral. And it only made her hungry for more.

The heat enveloping her and the ache he'd instilled deep inside her increased. Desperation rushed through her veins. She needed him to touch her just a little bit more to the left. Shifting her feet, she sought additional pressure, and sighed when she found what she needed.

A growl filled the air and then Callum muttered a curse. He grabbed her by the hips, effectively stilling her movements.

"Emily," he warned, his voice roughened by his raspy breaths. "We should stop before this gets out of hand."

"It's already out of hand, wouldn't you say?"

"Only a little," he muttered. "You've not yet got your skirts up around your waist and I've not undone my placket."

She tried to draw him back to her but he was a hard man to budge. Exasperated, she told him, "We're to be married, are we not?"

He drew back farther and his nostrils flared. Eyes filled with endless desire pierced hers. "I want you, Emily, make no mistake about it, but I'll not disgrace you in a folly while your relatives plan your grandmother's funeral."

The words had the same effect as dropping her into an icy pond. She stiffened with a horrified wince. "How could I let myself get carried away like that when she's…? Good Lord, I'm a terrible person."

"No, you're not." He pulled her into his arms and hugged her, then dropped a kiss to the top of her head. "I think we can both agree that we got a bit carried away."

"Thankfully one of us had the good sense to stop. My goodness, you must think me an absolute wanton."

"Certainly," he said with a grin. "But that's not a bad thing."

She elbowed him in the ribs as soon as he released her. "You're not supposed to admit to such things."

"Why on earth not?" he challenged. Grabbing her hand, he spun her back into his arms and kissed her again with possessive force. "You are to be my wife, Emily, so let's be perfectly clear. The way you responded to me just now makes me long for our wedding night more than you can imagine. I want you to be improper when we're together. It heats my blood, knowing how much you crave my touch. And just so you know, I look forward to doing all sorts of scandalous things with you in our bedroom."

"Good heavens." She patted her cheeks which had grown blazing hot. "Do all engaged couples speak so candidly with each other?"

"I've no idea," Callum said. He linked her arm with his and started guiding her back out into the sunshine. "It's simply how I intend to speak with you, and I do hope you will reciprocate. Being open and honest about our desires is, in my opinion, the way to ensure a happy marriage."

Emily pondered that for a moment before sending Callum a smug smile. "Well, in that case, you probably ought to know that I'd very much like to..." She rose up onto her toes and whispered the rest in his ear.

Callum suddenly coughed. When Emily drew back she saw that his eyes were impossibly wide. "I'm starting to think a special license might be in order."

"Oh no," said Emily, feigning dismay. "We mustn't dismiss the crying of banns without a good cause."

"You've just provided excellent cause," Callum muttered.

"Not so much fun, being tortured, is it?"

"Don't worry," he told her slyly while leading her back to the house. "I'll find a way to repay you, beginning with..."

The words *he* whispered next made Emily stumble. "That's not really a thing, is it?"

"I don't know. Is it?" He chuckled with devilish delight. "I'll let you know once you've done that other thing you just mentioned."

She punched him in the shoulder. "Impossible scoundrel."

"Delightful vixen."

Pursing her lips, she gave him a very unladylike sideways nudge, in response to which he picked her up and spun her around. Improprieties aside, he'd done what she'd asked of him in terms of cheering her up. It was exactly what she'd needed and left no doubt in her mind that he was much more than the Duke of Stratton, the man she'd decided to marry. He had become her dearest friend.

Nothing could possibly ruin that.

Or so she believed, until she returned home two days later and found the review she'd written for *Seductive Scandal* missing.

CHAPTER FIFTEEN

Callum had no doubt his marriage to Emily would be a smashing success. During the last few days, their relationship had been severely tested. They'd gotten engaged, fallen out with each other, mourned the loss of her grandmother, and made up.

Not only had they found their way through all of that together, but Callum believed they'd come out stronger. The connection they shared, because they'd had to deal with these difficult challenges, was one that couldn't be broken.

Happy in the knowledge she would become his wife, he returned home with a much lighter heart than when he'd left. He'd spoken with her parents before departing Seaton Hall. A hasty marriage by special license was off the table.

For starters, a mourning period was required. Emily's parents refused to accept anything less than three months. This, they claimed, would also allow enough time for the crying of banns and to make arrangements for the big day, which would include a respectably large wedding breakfast.

Callum hadn't argued too much, despite his impatience. He understood that a respectable amount of distance would be necessary between yesterday's funeral and the happy occasion. Plus, Emily was Lord and Lady Rosemont's only child. Of course they'd want to plan a big celebration when she married.

Peter greeted Callum when he entered the foyer.

"How was it?" he asked while Callum removed his hat and gloves.

Callum pondered how to answer that question and eventually settled on, "I'm glad I went."

"Did you hug her like I suggested."

"Yes," Callum said, unable to keep from smiling.

"And did it help her feel better?"

"I believe so."

"That's good." Peter dropped his gaze for a second before saying, "Now that you're back, I was wondering if you might show me how to fly the kite you bought me."

Callum's heart squeezed. He'd purchased the kite a month ago. Until now, Peter had completely dismissed it. It was good to see him showing an interest in pastime activities, and in spending more time together.

"We can certainly try. Our success will depend on the wind. But first, before we go, there's something I'd like your help with."

"Really?" Peter's eyes widened with interest.

"Come with me." Callum led the way to his study. Once inside, he gestured for Peter to close the door. "You can't share this with anyone, all right?"

Peter nodded. "I promise."

"Very well then." Having crossed to one of two bookcases filling the room, Callum retrieved a large wooden box that sat on the top shelf. He brought the box to his desk and opened the lid to reveal a wide selection of gemstones set into various pieces of jewelry.

"Blimey." Peter stared at the twinkling stones.

"Our task is of the utmost importance," Callum told him, deliberately infusing a conspiratorial note to his voice. "We must select the future Duchess of Stratton's engagement ring."

"That won't be easy," Peter muttered.

Callum rather agreed. The five options were equally splendid, but he'd have to pick one. Having proposed four days ago, it didn't sit well with him that Emily still didn't have his ring on her finger.

"How about this one?" Callum asked, holding up a diamond ring. It was simple but elegant.

"Very pretty," Peter agreed.

Callum frowned and set the ring back before picking up another containing rubies. "Or this one?"

"That's also very pretty."

"You're supposed to be helping me, Peter."

The boy rubbed the back of his neck. "All right. How about that one, to match her eyes."

Callum selected the one with a square cut emerald flanked by diamonds. He smiled. "It's absolutely perfect."

"Will you give it to her today?" Peter asked.

"That's my intention." Callum placed the ring inside his jacket pocket and returned the jewelry box to the shelf. "I'm not sure Emily will have returned home yet since she went by carriage. It will probably be another hour until she arrives, so why don't you and I go to the park in the meantime. We can stop by her house later on the way home."

"That's a brilliant idea. I'll go fetch the kite."

Callum chuckled. "Take your time, Peter. Don't trip on the stairs. I need ten minutes to freshen up too."

They arrived in the park after a brisk walk and found an open area without any trees for the kite to get tangled in.

"You'll want to hold it like this," Callum instructed. He gave a quick demonstration first, then passed the kite to Peter and adjusted his grip. "Don't unwind the spool too much. Keep it taut as you try to get the kite airborne. You can always add more length later."

"Which way do I run?"

"In the same direction as the wind." Callum stilled for a second to gauge the airflow, then pointed toward his right. "That way. Once you feel the wind starting to pull the kite out of your hand, you release it and unwind the spool."

Peter knit his brow as though in deep concentration, lifted the kite as Callum had shown him, and started to run. Callum watched as the kite started to flutter. Peter released it and turned with hope and excitement in his young eyes, only to watch as the kite lost momentum and drifted toward the ground.

"Try again," Callum told him. "Maybe hold the kite a bit higher."

Peter did as Callum suggested but once again, the kite dipped to the ground instead of rising.

"This is impossible," Peter muttered.

"It's rare to excel at something on your first try," Callum said. "Took me several go's when I was your age before I was able to get my kite into the air. You've got to keep at it if you want to succeed."

He watched as Peter walked back to his starting position, held the kite as he'd been instructed, and started running again.

"Are you sure you taught me the right way?" Peter asked after three more failed attempts.

"Yes," Callum assured him, "but it does require practice, and the wind today is a bit too gentle. We can always come back tomorrow. What's important is that you do not give up."

Peter huffed a breath and considered the kite. "One more try then."

Callum wished him luck and prayed Peter's efforts would be met with success. Arms crossed as he stood to one side, he tracked the boy's movements when he started running. "Yes, that's it. Faster, Peter. Keep going. Now release!"

The boy followed Callum's command and the kite began rising upward.

"Unwind the spool," Callum shouted, not caring that he was behaving without the slightest trace of decorum. "Slow and steady."

"I did it," Peter laughed as the kite rose even higher.

Grinning, Callum ran across the grass to where he stood. "Well done, lad."

He placed one hand on the boy's shoulder and stared up at the sky where the kite now twisted and twirled in response to the wind.

"Can we still come back tomorrow?" Peter asked when they gathered the kite a bit later and rewound its spool. "Even though I managed to do it today?"

"You've gotten a taste for it now, eh?"

"It's fun."

"I agree, and to answer your question, of course we can come back tomorrow."

Peter beamed. He looked mighty proud as he carried the kite along when they left the park. Callum could not be more pleased. He knew how important each small success was in life. Especially after a crippling experience.

Having exited the park, they started along Park Lane and continued toward Mount Street. They were just nearing Rosemont House when Callum spotted Emily who was hastening toward them from the opposite direction. She was alone, Callum noted, and a look of panic strained her features.

His pulse quickened with apprehension and he instantly lengthened his stride in order to reach her faster.

She spotted him in the next second and hurried to meet him.

"What's wrong?" he asked when she came to a halt before him. His hand caught her arm in a show of support. Whatever had happened, he'd help her through it.

"I scarcely know where to begin." Her voice was strained, her gaze darting about as though she herself sought some means of escape.

"Where's Georgina? Why isn't she with you?"

"What?" Emily finally focused on him, allowing him a glimpse of the turbulent angst in her eyes. She blinked and looked around as though surprised to find Georgina missing. "I was in such a hurry to speak with you, I must have forgotten to ask her to join me."

Callum glanced in the direction from which she'd

come. "Are you saying you went to my house without taking your chaperone with you?"

"Your butler said you were out."

Callum grew increasingly worried. It was unlike her to leave home unescorted. He steered her toward Rosemont House's front door while making sure Peter followed. "Let's go inside, Emily. You look like you could do with a soothing cup of tea."

Or perhaps something stronger, he decided when he realized her hands were shaking.

Whatever had happened, it had to be dire. She wasn't the sort of woman who needed smelling salts or whose nerves unraveled when faced with adversity. Emily was made of sturdier stuff. Seeing her like this made him worry another relation of hers might have died.

He ushered them into her home and directed her toward the parlor before addressing her butler. Unlike the previous time when he'd called, the man appeared more amicable, most likely because of Emily's presence.

"Lady Emily is feeling a little unwell," Callum said. "Can you please make sure a tea tray is brought up and that her lady's maid is informed. If it's not too much trouble, I'd also appreciate it if my ward is able to spend some time with Heidi while Lady Emily and I speak. He's very fond of her."

The butler's expression remained carefully

schooled. "I trust you'll leave the parlor door wide open until a maid joins you?"

"Of course," Callum assured him, adding a glower on account of the man suggesting he might be up to no good.

"Very well." The butler lowered his gaze to Peter. "Come with me, young man. Heidi was in the servant's hall having her fur combed, last I checked. There might be some cake for you too if you ask Cook nicely."

Reassured that the man in whose care he'd left Peter was not as severe as he appeared, Callum breathed a sigh of relief and entered the parlor. Emily, he saw, was pacing back and forth in front of the fireplace while wringing her hands. Seeing him, she came to a halt, even as she remained in restless motion. Biting her lip, she fidgeted with her skirts.

"I've done something terrible," Emily told him. She shook her head. "I don't know how you'll ever forgive me."

Callum went to her and took her hands gently between his own. He smoothed his thumbs over her skin in an effort to calm her. "Whatever it is, I'm sure it's not that bad."

She wasn't the malicious type. If she'd done something she believed he'd be angry about, it would be accidental. Callum was certain of this. The pained look in her eyes confirmed it.

"No," she whispered, her voice so small it clawed

at his heart. "It's worse."

Georgina entered at that exact moment, bringing a tea tray with her. Callum waited until she'd arranged the tea things and removed herself to her usual spot at the opposite end of the room, before guiding Emily to the sofa.

"Let's have some tea," he suggested, "and then we'll talk."

He urged Emily toward the spot on the far right of the sofa, then claimed the one on the left for himself. She served the tea and they each took a sip.

"Better?" Callum inquired.

"A little," she said even though she still looked as though she'd like to leap from the nearest window.

He took a deep breath and angled himself toward her. "Emily, whatever you've done, please know that it won't affect how I feel about you."

She shook her head. "How can you say such a thing when you don't know what it is yet?"

"Telling me would probably be a good start." He took another casual sip of his tea, attempting to look as non-threatening as possible.

She followed suit, then snatched up a biscuit, which she proceeded to eat with a striking degree of gusto. "I now know how you must have felt when you realized the threat your writing posed to our relationship. It's this horrible dread that's manifested behind my breastbone. It's an unbelievably wretched sensation."

"Emily," he said, firming his voice a little. "It won't go away until you confront the situation head-on. Tell me what happened and maybe I can help fix it."

"I don't see how. The man I spoke with said it was already too late."

"Man?" Callum tilted his head and frowned. "What man?"

"The one I spoke with at *The Mayfair Chronicle*. I went straight there when I realized what had happened. I explained to him that—"

"Emily." Callum set the palm of his hand against her cheek, forcing her gaze to meet his. "What did you do?"

"I... I wrote a review." Tears welled in her eyes. "You have to understand, Callum. I was hurt and angry at the time."

Callum's heart knocked back and forth with unsteady beats. "What did the review say?"

"That *Seductive Scandal* wasn't worth the paper on which it was printed and that I'd struggled to finished it. It's due to appear in tomorrow's paper."

He stared at her. She'd been right to worry. This was so much worse than what he'd expected. But he couldn't fault her for it. She'd responded in pain, but that didn't make her action less damning or hurtful. Least of all when considering all that had happened during the course of the last few days.

"I don't understand." If *The Mayfair Chronicle*

already had the review, she must have given it to them before departing for Seaton Hall. Before their conversation in the garden. Before their spectacular kiss. "How could you do this to me and then say that you love me?"

It wounded him more than he'd ever admit.

She shook her head. "I never intended to send it."

"And yet it still ended up at the printers." Try as he might, he couldn't quite keep the accusatory tone from his voice.

"By accident, Callum. I wrote it in anger, then left it on my desk." Emily sent her maid a quick look and lowered her voice to a whisper. "Georgina found it while I was away and thought I'd forgotten to have it delivered, so she did so herself. It's not unusual. She often delivers reviews on my behalf."

Callum stared at her and heaved a sigh. "We have to tell the others."

"Westcliffe and Corwin?" she asked with a note of dread.

"Exactly so. That book you've written a harsh critique of was meant to provide an income. As you know, I'm not financially secure, but neither are they. We were counting on that book to provide us enough funds so we might invest in profitable enterprises and grow our wealth."

"And I've wrecked it," Emily croaked.

Callum considered her sorry appearance. What was the point in agreeing with her when she clearly felt bad enough as it was? Besides, she'd only done it in response to his own actions. If she were to blame then perhaps so was he.

"All that matters now is stopping the publication."

"I tried to do so, Callum. It was the first thing I did before going in search of you."

"We have to go back and try harder." Callum stood. He swiped his jaw with his hand and attempted to gather his thoughts. He glanced at Emily. "Is your father home?"

"I believe he's in his study."

"Good." The earl was both well connected and wealthy, which could prove useful in this situation. "I want you to speak with him. Tell him what's happened. Do not omit a single detail. Explain to him how important it is that we fix this. I'm going to call on Westcliffe and Corwin in the meantime. We'll meet you at the newspaper in about half an hour. *Please* make sure your father comes with you."

"What's your plan?" Emily asked as she too stood, the anxiousness in her eyes so sharp it cut straight through him.

"To add some pressure." Callum headed for the door, speaking as he went. "It's not yet four in the afternoon. If they're refusing to pull the review, it's only because they're being stubborn."

CHAPTER SIXTEEN

Emily wanted to crawl into a hole and die. She'd never felt worse in her life. It didn't matter that her review had ended up at *The Mayfair Chronicle* by accident. She'd still written it. And then she'd left it on her desk where Georgina could easily find it.

Stupid. Stupid. Stupid.

She stared out of the carriage window as she and her father headed toward the newspaper office. What she'd done to Callum was worse than what he'd done to her. It had a far more calamitous effect. Not just on him, but on Westcliffe, Ada, Corwin, and Harriet.

Pressing her lips together, she did her best to maintain her composure. How would her friends ever forgive her? How would Callum be able to marry her, knowing this was how she responded in anger?

"I'm such a hypocrite," she muttered.

"Beg your pardon?" Papa asked.

She turned away from the window and faced him. "Remember how angry I was with Callum when I learned of what he had written? How am I any better when I did the exact same thing to him? I used words as a weapon, Papa. Except in my case it's so much worse because I deliberately aimed to hurt him. All he wanted to do was publish a story. And apparently, if I had taken the time to finish the book, I would have realized I was wrong to get upset over it. He used our history as inspiration. That's all. The only possible damage he could have caused was to my pride, whereas I've destroyed the chance he and two other families had of financial success."

"You're right to chastise yourself for what you did," Papa said. "It was spiteful. I'd not have thought you capable of it had you not told me about it yourself. So I can understand if Stratton is angry and possibly your friends too when they find out what's happened. You let emotion get the better of you, Emily, and in so doing you made a decision that threatens to have a terrible impact upon their lives."

"As if I didn't feel bad enough already," Emily mumbled.

Papa leaned forward and reached for her hand. "Let's hope there's a way out of this mess. Either way, my advice to you is to let them all know how sorry you are. Apologize profusely. Tell them you made a terrible error in judgement and pray they will forgive you. Then finish reading the book and write the review it deserves."

Emily nodded. It wasn't much different from what she herself had been planning, but hearing her father say it strengthened her resolve.

The carriage pulled up in front of *The Mayfair Chronicle*. Papa alit and Emily followed him down onto the pavement. When they entered the front office, Callum was already there with the two other dukes. The three men greeted Emily and her father with grim expressions before returning their attention to the clerk with whom they'd been speaking. He was the same one Emily had spoken with earlier.

"It's not so simple, Your Grace," the clerk was saying, his voice holding the apologetic tone of someone who'd just received a sound reprimanding. "As I explained to your um—"

"Fiancée," Callum provided, his words a wonderful reassurance to Emily. They were still getting married. He wasn't so angry he'd break the engagement.

"Right. Um..." The clerk cleared his throat and sent Emily a wary glance. "As I explained to her this morning, publishing is a carefully scheduled process. One cannot remove columns or articles at the last second. The layout for tomorrow's publication will already have been prepared."

"But you do make exceptions," Callum said, his voice filled with dukely authority. "For when something newsworthy happens."

"Last night's theft at Coldweather House would not have made this morning's paper otherwise," Emily said, stepping forward to stand beside Callum. "As I recall, that transpired after nine o'clock."

"Well yes," said the clerk. "News is naturally treated with the utmost of urgency."

"Yet you refuse to remove a review written in error," Callum told him. "Consider the impact such a decision will have on your publication."

"I beg your pardon?"

Callum reached for Emily's hand and gave it a squeeze before letting it go once more. "The Lady Librarian is a popular column, is it not?"

"I'm really not qualified to discuss that," said the clerk.

"Then maybe you can fetch us someone who is."

"Like the owner and editor-in-chief, Mr. Loughton," Papa suggested

The clerk's face reddened. "He's an incredibly busy man, sir."

"That's, my lord, to you." Papa raised his chin.

Callum leaned forward. "I'm sure Mr. Loughton can make time for three dukes and an earl. Wouldn't you say?"

"I…um…ah…Of course." The clerk took a step back. "I'll let him know you're here at once."

He nearly tripped over his feet in his sudden haste to get the job done.

"This is nonsense," Westcliffe muttered.

Corwin nodded. "I'll be ending my subscription before we leave."

"I'm so sorry," Emily told them. "I'm sure Callum has briefed you on what happened."

"He did," Westcliffe said without adding anything further.

Corwin said nothing. He didn't even look at her, which almost made her feel worse than Westcliffe's scowl.

"I'll find a way out of this mess one way or the other," she promised, even though she had no idea how or where to begin. Hopefully speaking with Mr. Loughton would be a good start.

The man arrived within the next minute. His expression, unlike the clerk's, was warm and hospitable. Emily's heart gave a hopeful beat.

"Welcome gentlemen." Mr. Loughton extended his hand to everyone in turn and introductions were hastily made. "To what do I owe this pleasure?"

"I believe I'll let my daughter explain," Papa told him.

Although Emily technically worked for Mr. Loughton, she'd never actually met him. All of her communication with the newspaper had taken place by letter. It was time for him to find out who she truly was.

"Mr. Loughton. My name is Emily Brooke, otherwise known as The Lady Librarian."

Mr. Loughton's eyes widened. He grinned. "How positively marvelous! My wife and I are both admirers of your writing. We read all your reviews and purchase our books accordingly."

"Thank you." Emily gave him a tight smile. "As I explained to your clerk, one of the reviews I wrote was delivered to you in error. It's scheduled to appear in tomorrow's paper, but if it does, it will discredit what I truly believe to be a wonderful novel."

Mr. Loughton frowned. "If that's your position, then why would you write a review to the contrary?"

"The reason is irrelevant in this instance. All that matters is that the review gets retracted with no damage done to the book's potential."

"I've got to tell you this is a bit last minute." Mr. Loughton scratched his head. "I'm not sure there's much to be done. The Lady Librarian's column is in the middle of the paper. It's placed in a spot where no changes are ever expected. Those pages get printed first, beginning at eight in the morning the day before publication. This allows us the extra time we need to work on the first few pages, where all the headlines appear, at the last minute."

"So what you're saying," Emily asked, just to be clear, "is that the page with The Lady Librarian's review has already been printed?"

"Probably."

"Can we check?" she asked, her panic from earlier returning in full force.

Mr. Loughton nodded. "Come with me."

They followed him into the back office area where a group of roughly twenty men were either busy at their desks or bustling about as though pressed for time.

Mr. Loughton approached a slim man with thinning blond hair. "Mr. Conrad. I need an update on tomorrow's edition. Has the page featuring The Lady Librarian been printed yet?"

"It was completed about an hour ago," Mr. Conrad informed his employer.

Mr. Loughton turned to Emily and the rest of the group, his expression apologetic. "I'm terribly sorry, but if it's already printed, there's nothing to be done."

Emily's heart sank like a big lump of lead. She didn't need to look at Callum to know what a terrible blow this was. She could feel his despair as though it were her own. Something had to be done. One way or another she had to find a way to make this right.

A thought struck.

"What would it cost to purchase all of those pages?" she asked.

Mr. Loughton drew back. He frowned. "I beg your pardon?"

"Emily," Papa murmured. "You're surely looking at more than fifty pounds here."

"I can't afford that right now," Callum told her, his voice grim.

"Neither can we," said Westcliffe and Corwin.

Maybe not. But *she* could.

"I'm guessing the only reason you're unable to pull the pages, is because it would be too expensive," she told Mr. Loughton. "I understand that. Paper isn't cheap. But what if I wished to purchase all of the pages with that review printed on them? How much would you charge me?"

Mr. Loughton's eyebrows shot toward his hairline. "I don't know. I'd have to make a calculation. But to be honest with you, my lady, I cannot afford to sell those pages. It's not just a question of money, you see, but also of time. We'd never be able to get the paper out by tomorrow morning if we have to re-print a replacement page this late in the day. Doing so would require reworking the layout since the objective is to remove the review. We'd have to find something of a similar size to fill the vacant spot."

"That's not a problem," Emily told him. "I'll just write a new review. One that fits the exact space left by the one we're removing."

"You haven't even read the entire book," Callum said.

"I don't need to." Emily turned to him with determination. After all he'd done to help her, she would do this. "It's written by you and your friends. Based on what I've read so far, I'm sure the entire story will be a delight. It's certainly a gamble I'm willing to take."

He looked skeptical. "Are you sure?"

"Without question. My initial review was written in anger, Callum. It never should have been read by anyone other than me."

"I appreciate your saying so," he said with a hint of being slightly reassured, "but it doesn't change the fact that we cannot afford to do as you suggest."

"And even if you could," Westcliffe said, "Mr. Loughton did just inform us that there's not enough time."

Yes. The time would likely prove to be the greatest challenge of all. Emily's mind whirled. She bit her lip and glanced at Corwin. "You're acquainted with a publisher, are you not?"

He raised his chin and rocked back on his heels. "I am."

"Any chance you might be able to convince him to print the page in question?"

"Possibly," Corwin said, his expression pensive.

"How long would it take for you to find out for certain and meet us back here?" Emily asked.

"An hour or so, I should think. Give or take."

Emily nodded. "Please do it."

"Hold on," Callum said. "There's no sense in

setting a huge undertaking in motion when we're not even able to pull the pages."

Emily turned to Mr. Loughton. "Can you please get me the price of those pages?"

Callum raised an eyebrow as though impressed by her persistence.

Well, she would not be giving up. This was too important.

Mr. Loughton and Mr. Conrad removed themselves to a desk where they proceeded to make some notes on a piece of paper. When they finished, Mr. Loughton approached her and said, "We're looking at four thousand pages at roughly one farthing a piece, plus the cost of replacement paper which more or less doubles the cost. By my estimation, that comes to roughly sixty-seven pounds."

He handed Emily the note on which he'd made his calculations. She glanced at it while doing her best not to look too shocked. It truly was a large sum.

Intent on staying optimistic, she sent Callum and his friends a reassuring smile before addressing her father. "Papa. A word in private, if you will?"

The earl followed her off to one side. "The pensive gleam in your eyes is making me nervous, Emily. What are you thinking?"

"I want to use my dowry."

Papa's face blanched. "Absolutely not."

"Listen to me, Papa. This terrible blunder is my

doing. I caused this and now I have to do what I can to atone. It's only fair."

"I don't like it." Papa crossed his arms. "Your dowry is intended to give you security, Emily."

"Most of it still will. I'll only be using a very small portion."

Papa knit his brow. "I'd rather cover the cost myself and leave your dowry alone."

"As generous as that is and as grateful as I am to you for the offer, it would not be the same." Emily glanced in Callum's direction. "Since I am the one to blame for what happened, I must be the one who pays the price."

"You know, there's no guarantee the book will make enough money to make up for this expense." Papa's voice was somber. "It might be cheaper to leave the review as is."

"Perhaps, but that doesn't help me make amends. I need to do this. Plus, having read part of the book, I actually do believe it will do quite well if enough people buy it. Ensuring its success will also help the next book they write."

"They're planning another?"

"I believe so. Yes." She took a deep breath and expelled it. "Papa, you must help me with this. Please. It's not just about the book. It's also about ensuring that I have a positive start to my marriage. This is extremely important to me. It would mean a great deal if you'd lend your assistance."

Papa sighed. "Very well, Emily. I will support you in this if it's what you desire."

Forgetting they were in a public setting, Emily wound her arms around her father and hugged him. "Thank you."

Papa murmured something beneath his breath and Emily withdrew. She crossed to where Callum and his friends waited together with Mr. Loughton.

"Corwin, if you can please proceed as we discussed, I'll pay to have the page pulled and replaced."

CHAPTER SEVENTEEN

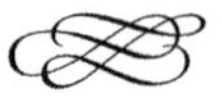

"I'll come with you," Anthony told Brody. The two men gave every assurance they would return as quickly as possible, then left.

Callum stared at Emily. "Are you mad?"

The sum Mr. Loughton had quoted was greater than he'd expected.

"No." Emily gazed at him with just as much heartache as he had endured when he'd realized the words he'd written would surely hurt her. "I simply recognize my mistake and know I have no choice but to do this. I'll never forgive myself otherwise, and will always worry you can't forgive me either."

"Emily." He took her hand and gave it a squeeze. "I made my own mistake so of course I'll forgive you. Especially since your actions were a direct result of my own."

"Possibly, but that doesn't change the fact that this is much worse than what you did."

"Knowing how much I hurt you, I have to disagree."

"Nevertheless, I have the chance to make it right and it's a chance I'm going to take."

"I still don't understand how." Callum glanced at the earl. "Is your father loaning the money?"

"In a sense. He'll give Mr. Loughton a cheque to guarantee payment and withdraw the sum from my dowry."

"You're using your dowry for this?" Callum could scarcely believe it. That money was meant to provide for her in case he failed to do so. That had been his agreement with her father, that the contract should be written in such a way she would retain sole right to the funds she brought to the marriage. "Emily, I cannot in good conscience let you do so."

Her gaze met his with unyielding directness. "Would you rather tomorrow's paper be sold as is? Imagine the impact that would have, not just on you but on Westcliffe and Corwin as well. On their families. They need this as much as you do."

Of course they did, but her sacrifice still seemed out of proportion compared with what she had done. Callum could scarcely credit it. Unfortunately, having wasted most of his fortune, he was unable to make the payment himself. Whatever funds he had at his disposal had to go toward servants' wages and bills. As such, he lacked the ability to stop her.

Dazed, he watched as her father wrote the cheque and handed it to Mr. Loughton. It twisted Callum's gut knowing Emily had to save him like this when he should be able to save her instead.

Somehow, he'd have to make this up to her, for despite her argument being that she owed him, he couldn't stop feeling like it was the other way around. He'd set all of this into motion. Had he simply applied a bit more common sense, they probably wouldn't be in this situation to begin with.

"Mr. Hudson says he can help," Brody said when he and Anthony returned some time later, both panting for breath. "Harriet will too. She'll need a copy of the page that's getting pulled, a newspaper-sized printing frame, paper, and the review that's supposed to replace the old one."

"I can provide the frame and the paper," Mr. Loughton said, proving himself more helpful now that he knew his expense would be covered.

"Is there a desk I can use?" Emily asked. "That way I can write the replacement review while the rest of the items are being prepared for delivery."

"You can use mine," said Mr. Conrad. "I'll see to acquiring the paper and the frame."

Emily thanked him as he departed and took her seat. She selected a piece of blank paper from a small stack and dipped the available quill in the inkwell.

Once finished, she re-read what she'd written a couple of times before handing it to Callum.

His pulse leapt as soon as he read the first line. *A novel that's sure to delight enthusiasts of Miss Austen's writing.* He glanced at Emily and saw the hope in her eyes. She bit her lip, betraying the uncertain depths of anxiety she experienced as she awaited his opinion.

"This is incredible," he whispered.

"Can I see?" Anthony asked. Callum handed him the review. "Filled with memorable characters, an engaging plot, and the sort of wit that will surely brighten your day, this marvelous debut of a novel reinforces the dream of a great romance. It is, without doubt, the sort of story one will want to re-read time and again, and one that I would highly recommend you purchase without further delay."

"That's quite the stamp of approval," Brody said. "Thank you, Emily."

"Yes," Anthony said. "Thank you."

"I scarcely know what to say," Callum told her. "If this review has the effect I believe it shall have, the book is bound to fly off the shelves when it goes on sale tomorrow."

"It is the least I could do," Emily told them as she set the quill aside and stood. "And just so you know, I believe I'll agree with every word I've just written once I finish reading the book. As I intend to do as soon as I return home."

Impulsively, Callum pulled her into his arms.

She squeaked but he ignored her as he dipped his head and pressed his mouth to hers. It didn't matter that they were standing in a busy office space and that he really ought to refrain from such an inappropriate show of affection. All that mattered was Emily and her feelings. It was imperative he prove to her that he did not harbor any ill feelings toward her, that he forgave her for what she'd done, and that they would be fine. She need not fear on that score.

So he hugged her close, squeezing her slightly against him while adding a bit more force to the kiss, just to be sure she understood him. They belonged together and no error in judgement, however great or small, would change that. Whatever mistakes either of them made in the future, they would get through it together.

Someone coughed and Callum grinned against her lips as he slowly withdrew, adding distance. The look in her eyes was one of confusion and wonder.

"Oh," was all she said, in response to which Callum almost kissed her again. She was simply too adorable.

"There will be time for that later," her father said. "*After* you speak your vows."

Three long months from now.

Callum sent the earl a disgruntled look only to note that he seemed to be forcing a frown in an effort to hide his amusement.

"He's right," Anthony said. He waved the piece of paper with the review. "There's work to be done at the moment and we've a schedule to keep if we're to succeed."

"I'll need the new pages by midnight, at the latest," Mr. Loughton informed them when Mr. Conrad returned. Three men followed him, each carrying bundles of newsprint while Mr. Conrad himself carried the frame.

"We'd best get on with it then," Brody said.

Callum agreed. They couldn't afford to waste a second. "I'll hail a hackney carriage so we can transport the items."

"We can use our carriage too if needed," Emily said. She glanced at her father. "Right, Papa?"

The earl agreed and the paper was loaded into both the Rosemont carriage and a hackney, leaving just enough room for two to three people in each. Callum travelled with Emily and her father while Anthony and Brody took the hackney.

"I need to return home once we've dropped off the paper," Rosemont said. "Friends will be calling to offer condolences on Lady Seaton's death. I'd rather not leave your mother alone with it, Emily."

"Of course. I understand." She clasped her hands together and worried her lip between her teeth before asking, "Will you permit me to stay at Hudson & Co? My friend, Harriet, the Duchess of

Corwin, will be there too, so I shan't be without a chaperone."

Rosemont's expression turned slightly more serious. He seemed to consider, and eventually nodded. "Provided you're home no later than ten. I'll send the carriage to pick you up."

"Thank you, Papa."

They arrived moments later and Callum alit first so he could help Emily down. He then held the door for her father. Anthony and Brody, who'd arrived a moment before, helped carry the paper around to the back of the print shop.

"I'll wish you luck," Rosemont said. He extended his hand to Callum, who instantly shook it. "Once this is over, I trust we'll get on with planning your wedding."

"I look forward to it," Callum told him.

Rosemont added a nod, reminded his daughter that he expected her home in four hours, and departed. A light and giddy sort of sensation spiraled through Callum's chest. He glanced at Emily, whose eyes brimmed with a mixture of uncertainty and excitement.

"I hope this works," she said.

"It will," he assured her. It did not escape his notice that they were the only two people who stood on the pavement. Everyone else had already vanished inside Hudson & Co. Callum reached for Emily's hand. This was as good a place as any for what he'd been waiting for most of the day. "There's something I wish to say before we go inside. When I proposed, I did so on a whim, without having an actual plan. It was a spur of the moment decision, and because of this, I wasn't as prepared as I ought to have been."

"Callum, if you have regrets, I completely understand. It was a game of pretend that got out of hand, so if you'd like to break off the engagement, I'm sure we can find a way." She produced a sad sort of chuckle. "I mean, if we can get *The Mayfair Chronicle* to change their paper's content at the last minute, anything is possible. Right?"

He stared at her, feeling a bit like she'd just grabbed his heart and yanked it sideways. "Is that what you want?"

"Of course not, Callum. I love you more than I thought I could ever love anyone. That's why this mess I've gotten us into is so incredibly hard for me to deal with."

"I forgive you for it. I do not blame you, so please stop blaming yourself. Can you do that?"

"I'll try, but it may take a while. I still feel awful."

"As do I," he confessed. "But I love you too and I don't want to end our engagement either. In fact, I'd like to make it official by giving you this."

He reached inside his jacket pocket and produced the ring he'd selected earlier. Gently holding her hand, he slipped it onto her finger.

"Oh..." she breathed. "It's absolutely stunning."

"Peter helped me select it." He admired the perfection with which it fit her finger. "Honestly, I had considered selling it and the rest of the jewels I've inherited from my grandmother. They would have solved my financial woes. Without an immediate plan to marry, I didn't think I'd be needing the jewelry any time soon. But now that you are to be my wife, the Duchess of Stratton, they shall be yours."

"Callum…"

He pulled her into his arms and kissed her fiercely before setting her back on her feet.

"I don't know what your father was thinking to leave you here in my care."

She grinned. "I'm sure he believes you're aware of the risk you'll be taking if you attempt something truly improper. His dueling pistols are his most prized possessions."

"You don't say," Callum muttered while taking a large theatrical step backward. "Best keep my distance then. Shall we?"

The warmth of her laughter as she preceded him inside the printers settled his nerves and assured him all would be well. The damning review would be replaced while he, the luckiest man in the world, would soon become Emily Brooke's husband.

Life was beginning to look a bit brighter.

CHAPTER EIGHTEEN

It was not yet seven o'clock when Emily rose the next morning. She'd not slept a wink. Instead, she'd spent the entire night reading the rest of the book Callum, Westcliffe, and Corwin had written. It was, she decided, an absolute treat.

Instead of heading to breakfast, she hurried downstairs to the kitchen.

"Has the paper arrived yet?" she asked a footman.

"I believe Larrow is pressing it right now."

Emily thanked the footman and continued toward the butler's pantry. She knocked on the door and pushed it open when Larrow's voice invited her to enter.

His eyes widened when he saw it was she, and he instantly drew to attention. "Good morning, my lady. How may I be of service?"

"Please take care not to burn that," Emily said,

noting that he'd released his hold on the iron and left it on top of the paper. "I'm very eager to read it."

"Of course." He snatched the iron back up. "I'll just be a moment."

Emily tried her best to remain as patient as possible while the butler finished his task, but could not refrain from tapping her foot.

"Sorry," she muttered when he sent her a curious look.

"Will you not go upstairs?" he asked. "I can bring it to you as soon as it's ready."

"Very well. Just don't take too long."

She removed herself to the dining room where a hot cup of tea provided a lovely distraction. The paper arrived the next moment, offered to her on a silver tray. Emily snatched it up with more haste than was deemed proper and promptly leafed to the only section of interest.

Relief sped through her veins when she saw the page Harriet had created. It was perfect. The old review was gone and in its place was the new one she'd written.

Emily re-folded the paper and placed it neatly beside her father's plate. She then downed the rest of her tea, quickly ate a slice of toast, and returned upstairs where Georgina helped her prepare for the day ahead. By eight-thirty, the two of them left the house and set their course for Hatchards.

The place didn't open until nine o'clock so they

were still a bit early. They were, however, not the only customers to have arrived. A queue was already forming. Since this was slightly unusual, Emily approached one of the ladies who waited for the doors to be opened.

"Excuse me," said Emily. "May I inquire as to your reason for having come here so early?"

"I love Miss Austen's novels," the woman informed her. "I've read every one and was very sad when I learned there wouldn't be any more. But apparently there's a new author who's writing similar stories. I just read the review, written by The Lady Librarian. Her opinion has never steered me wrong, so I'm hopeful this story will be compelling. I thought it best to arrive in good time in case others were of a similar notion."

Apparently, they were, Emily decided. The line had increased in length during the brief time in which the woman had spoken. Emily thanked her and moved to the end of the queue where she was able to get a similar opinion from another customer.

Rejoicing at the immediate hint of success the book was getting, she did her best to keep from grinning too much. By the time she entered the bookshop, only a few editions of the book remained. She refrained from taking one for herself since she already had a copy.

Instead, she left the shop with Georgina and headed toward Between the Pages, the bookshop owned by Ada's uncle. The lovely aroma from the next-door bakery tempted her to stop there first and purchase a bag full of raisin buns. She offered one to Georgina before venturing inside the bookshop. Much like Hatchard's, it was packed with customers.

Ada's uncle, Mr. Quinn, was in the process of wrapping an order for one of the many women filling the space.

"Thank you so much," the woman said when Mr. Quinn handed over her parcel. "Taylor & Jones over on Dean Street was already sold out. I'm so relieved to have found a copy here."

"I hope you enjoy the story," Mr. Quinn told her. "And should you wish for it to be properly bound, simply return with your receipt and we'll give you a discount."

The lady thanked him and departed.

Leaving Georgina by the door, Emily approached the counter. "I'm happy to lend a hand if you need a break."

Mr. Quinn's mouth slanted as he wrapped another copy of *Seductive Scandal* in brown paper. "I can't believe the speed with which this book is selling. It's unlike anything I've seen before. The customers don't even want to wait for the book to be bound. They just want the pages so they can start reading at once."

Emily set down her parcel of buns and helped the next lady in line.

"I hope you enjoy the story," Emily told her.

"Oh, if the hero is anything like Mr. Darcy, I'm sure I'll love every moment." The rest of the women who stood behind her voiced their agreement.

Emily chuckled and wished her a pleasant day before helping the next customer with her purchase.

She bid Mr. Quinn farewell a half hour later and walked to Pall Mall. There, she stopped by an additional bookshop before taking a hackney to Westcliffe House. It was not her preferred destination of course, but as a young unmarried woman, she ought not stop by Stratton House without bringing her parents.

When she'd done so yesterday she'd been too beside herself to think of the possible repercussions.

"The book is a splendid success," she told Ada when they met in the Westcliffe parlor. "The bookshops are already selling out."

"I thought it might be a busy day after reading the splendid review you wrote," Ada said. "It's my intention to go help my uncle this afternoon."

"Too late for that," Emily told her. "He's already sold every copy of *Seductive Scandal* he had in supply."

"You're joking."

"Not at all."

"But the shops have only been open for a couple of hours."

"What can I say?" Emily grinned. "The book your

husband wrote with his friends is a smashing success."

"How marvelous." Ada gave Emily a hug. "I'm sure it's thanks to you."

"Absolutely not. Several customers read the first pages before choosing to purchase a copy. Had the writing not been up to par, they'd not have done so, no matter how good my review might have been."

"Am I to understand there's good news?" Westcliffe asked as he sauntered into the parlor. "Your squeals and laughter were audible from the dining room so I trust there's cause for some celebration?"

"The book is selling out," Ada told him with a wide grin.

His expression brightened. "You don't say."

"I was actually wondering if you'd be willing to ask Corwin and Stratton to join us," Emily said. "I'd like to let them both know, but I cannot stop by Stratton House on my own."

"Of course." Westcliffe rang for the butler and issued instructions for both of his friends to be summoned, along with Corwin's wife, Harriet. "And please ask Cook to prepare a feast for luncheon. Given the hour, I believe my friends will be staying to eat."

Emily counted the minutes after the butler's departure. She could not stop from checking the clock, which appeared to be moving at a snail's pace.

"Have you decided on where you're going to have the wedding?" Ada asked.

"Not really." Emily took a sip of the tea she'd been served. "So much has happened since we decided to marry, I've not found the time."

"Of course." Ada placed her hand over Emily's. "Anthony and I were both extremely sorry to hear of your grandmother's death. That must have been terribly hard."

"Yes. It was very sudden." A solemn moment of silence followed. Finding it stifling, Emily chose to say, "I think St. George's would be lovely, if Callum agrees."

"I've always liked that church," Anthony said. "It's a good size – not overwhelmingly large."

"Exactly," Emily agreed. "When I get home I'll start putting together a guest list. Mama will likely want to be involved, especially with regard to the wedding breakfast. And then, I suppose, I should visit a modiste."

"I'd love to come with you," Ada said. "I'm sure Harriet would as well. We could make a day of it, if you like, with luncheon at Mivart's."

"What a lovely idea." Emily glanced at the clock again and saw that only ten minutes had passed since the last time she'd checked. Returning her attention to her friends, she said, "The next book club meeting is set to take place this coming Saturday. I'm thinking of suggesting *Seductive Scandal* as the monthly novel."

"Yes," Ada agreed. "If some of the members have not yet read the book, this will get them to do so, which should improve on word-of-mouth sales."

"But if the book is sold out," Anthony mused, "will you not risk making it difficult for them to get their hands on a copy?"

"Perhaps we can use our copies. I believe we have three between us. Callum has one too, so that's four editions we could potentially lend. Besides which, I can check with the printer to see if it's possible to have additional copies printed upon request."

"It's possible they'll publish a second edition based on success," Ada said, "but that does tend to happen a few months later."

"Callum did mention the possibility of your writing a second book with Emilia Parker and Mr. Dalton as the main characters. What's your opinion on that?"

"I'm happy to give it a go," Anthony said. "Working with Brody and Callum on this was actually a very enjoyable experience. I'd like to do it again."

"Speaking of which," Emily said. "Have the three of you not considered naming yourselves as joint authors?"

"Not really."

"Why not?"

"Well for one thing, *Seductive Scandal* is a romance novel. Everyone will expect a woman to be the author."

"Precisely." Emily tilted her head in thought. "I believe your books would be even *more* sought after if it were known they were written by three men."

"I don't know." Anthony glanced at Ada. "What do you think?"

"In my opinion, you and your friends deserve the credit, so it's only if you wish to remain anonymous for the sake of privacy that you should keep your names secret. Otherwise, I do think Emily may have a point. It may even encourage men to purchase the book."

"Exactly." Emily leaned forward. "All the customers I saw today at the bookshops were women. But if the authors were known to be men, men might want to read the story too. And this could make the second edition sell out as well, which would lead to a third edition, perhaps even a fourth. It's certainly worth thinking about. Is it not?"

"Indeed," Anthony murmured, his expression pensive.

The sound of the front door opening and closing made Emily still even as her heart gave a swift series of hops. She glanced at the door and jerked to her feet when it opened to admit Brody and Harriet, followed by Callum.

His warm gaze met hers, weakening her knees to

such a degree that she wobbled a little. He must have noticed for there was a blatant degree of amusement in his eyes, not to mention a touch of male satisfaction. It was patently clear that he liked the effect he was having on her.

She couldn't blame him. It pleased her too when she stepped toward him and saw he wasn't quite as composed as he tried to let on. The pulse beating at his throat betrayed him.

"Callum," she whispered, forgoing all manner of etiquette. She gave him a broad smile. "The book is a smashing success. Every shop I visited on my way here is already sold out, including Hatchards."

He grinned alongside Brody and Harriet.

"That's marvelous news!" And then, as though it were just the two of them and they'd been married for years, he swept her into his arms and spun her around. "Thank you, my love. It appears as though your review has paid off."

"Only because you and your friends wrote a wonderful book."

His eyes held hers. "It would not have had this kind of success without your assistance."

"I've just been discussing the idea of having the book club read it next month. This will help spread the word even more. As would revealing the true identities of the authors. If you and your friends agree, we could host an author event where the book club members get a chance to discuss the book with you."

"That's quite a lot to consider," Brody said.

"Agreed." Callum, who still held Emily in his arms with complete disregard for propriety, drew her even closer. "We'll have to discuss it. But first, there's something more pressing for me to address."

Before she was able to wonder what that might be, he captured her mouth with his in a searing kiss that completely stole her breath. All she could do was cling to him while their friends clapped and cheered as though all of this were perfectly normal. Then again, none of them were remotely normal. They were three penniless dukes attempting to earn an income, a bookshop owner's niece, a woman who'd made her living dressed as a boy, and The Lady Librarian.

Appreciating the love and friendship filling the room, Emily kissed Callum back with fervor while counting the days to their wedding.

CHAPTER NINETEEN

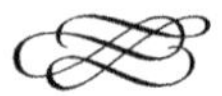

It was a crisp February day when Emily left for St. George's, but at least the sun was shining. The golden light reflected off the thin sheen of frost that covered the pavement and clung to the fences, producing a shimmery fairy-tale sparkle.

Seated beside her father, with a hot brick at her feet, Emily appreciated the light blue wool frock dress she'd ordered for the occasion. Fashioned from worsted wool and trimmed with white fur, it offered more warmth than she would have found had she chosen to dress in silk.

It had been her mother's idea and while Emily had been opposed to begin with, she'd changed her mind when Callum had seen the sketch and voiced his approval. With her stomach tight on account of the nerves that had made her feel slightly ill since last night, Emily fidgeted with the ring Callum had given her.

"Take a deep breath," Papa said, his voice conveying a touch of amusement. "I can feel the tension wafting off you."

She did as he suggested, then sighed. "I'm sorry, but it cannot be helped. My life is about to change in front of a whole crowd of people."

"If you've changed your mind about marrying him, we can—"

"Of course not. I love him, Papa. Becoming his wife is all I've been able to think of these past few weeks."

"Then focus on that." Papa took her hand and gave it a squeeze. "Focus on the man who's waiting for you at the end of the aisle and know he will most certainly be just as nervous as you. If not more so."

Emily followed her father's advice some ten minutes later, her attention fixed solely on Callum. Dressed in a navy-blue frock coat, cream-colored trousers, and a light blue waistcoat embroidered with silver thread, he looked unbelievably dashing. He also appeared extremely impatient and slightly anxious, just as Papa had suggested he would.

His sigh, when she reached him, seemed to confirm this, as did the hitch to his voice when he whispered, "I truly am the luckiest man in the world."

Blinking back tears of emotion, Emily croaked

out, "I'm lucky too," while accepting the arm he offered. Together, they stepped up to the altar and faced the priest.

What followed felt like an endless series of prayers and hymns. Emily's mind wandered more than once. She wondered how their wedding night might proceed. What should she wear? Her trousseau consisted of three appropriate items, but which one would Callum prefer? She chastised herself for considering such things while standing in church and dragged her attention back to the priest and what he was saying.

"…so long as you both shall live?"

"Yes," Emily nearly shouted when she realized she was the one being addressed.

A soft chuckle beside her suggested that Callum had realized what must have occurred.

"I found it hard to concentrate too," he told her later as they rode toward Rosemont House. The wedding breakfast would be held there, after which Emily and Callum would continue onward to Stratton House. Peter, it had been decided, would remain with Emily's parents overnight, allowing the newlyweds time for themselves.

"Is it just me or did it feel as though that particular service took longer than usual?"

"It's not just you," he said with a grin right before leaning in to press a hot kiss to her cheek. "As far as I was concerned, it could not end soon enough.

Neither can this wedding breakfast, by the way. I find it to be a ghastly tradition."

Emily smiled even as her cheeks flushed in response to him setting his hand on her thigh. "I think we'd both regret not celebrating with our family and friends."

"We could easily do so tomorrow." He waggled his eyebrows.

"Would you like to suggest that to our parents?" She'd met his mother a couple of months earlier, and although the lady was slightly peculiar, it was clear that she loved her son enormously. The wedding had become something of a hobby for her. She'd helped Emily's mother plan the menu and order floral arrangements.

Callum choked. "I'd rather not."

"Don't look at me," Emily told him when his expression turned pleading.

"Fine," Callum muttered. He knit his brow, then promptly opened the window and leaned out so he could call to the driver. "Take us on a ten-minute detour."

"What are you doing?" Emily chuckled while pulling him back inside the carriage.

"Giving us something to help tide us over." He reached for her, his arm winding around her waist as he pulled her into his lap. "There. Much better."

Emily laughed. "I wasn't aware you were such a scoundrel."

His eyes darkened. "You haven't seen anything yet."

She gasped when his hand crept under her skirts. Holding her gaze, he allowed his fingers to toy with her ankle for a brief moment before sliding them slightly higher.

Emily clutched at his shoulders.

"You're my wife now, Emily. I no longer need to stop."

Heat engulfed her as understanding dawned. His mouth met hers and he kissed her with ravenous hunger, turning her body into an inferno of need.

True to his word, her husband continued showing her what she had to look forward to later. And when she eventually sagged against him with euphoric bliss, he whispered a promise right next to her ear. "There's so much more to come, I can scarcely wait to show you."

Standing by the sideboard in his parlor, Callum poured two glasses of port. The wedding breakfast had not been as tedious as he had feared. In fact, he'd rather enjoyed it, though he reckoned his indiscretion with Emily in the carriage had much to do with that. Watching her come apart in his arms had appeased him a little. For weeks, he'd wondered what that would be like, and now he knew. It was glorious.

He crossed to where she sat. Although her eyes were bright with happiness and expectation, she looked like someone attempting to feign confidence when they were truly quite anxious. The port would help. He handed it to her and clinked his glass against hers before taking a seat on the sofa beside her.

"To our future happiness," he murmured.

She echoed the toast and sipped her drink. "Your house is lovely, by the way. Did I mention that yet?"

"You did." He'd given her a tour of the downstairs, but had yet to show her the bedchambers.

"I look forward to exploring the library more and to playing the pianoforte. A house is most homely when filled with music, don't you think?"

"It is," he agreed while observing her stiff posture, the high color in her cheeks, and the way her fingers were clutching the glass. She took another sip of her drink.

What Callum truly wanted to do was get her upstairs and out of her clothes, but she still didn't look quite ready for that. If he suggested it, he worried she'd just get more nervous. He pondered their situation. They were both on the sofa. The servants had been sent away. No one was going to walk in on them.

He downed the remainder of his drink and set

his glass aside. "Do you like this particular port or do you prefer a sweeter variety?"

"Oh, this one is very good." She drank some more and licked her lips. "It has a wonderfully soothing effect as well. I rather like it."

"I was thinking we might go skating tomorrow," Callum suggested while lazily placing his arm across the back of the sofa so he could stroke his thumb over the back of her neck. "You do skate, do you not?"

"Of course I do," Emily said. She expelled an almost imperceptible sigh while leaning back into his subtle caress. "I enjoy it tremendously."

"Excellent." He shifted a little bit closer and placed one hand on her thigh, just as he'd done in the carriage. The fingers brushing the nape of her neck slid sideways to toy with a bit of fur trim at her shoulder before dipping underneath the edge of her gown to brush hidden skin. "We'll have tea and cake at Gunther's after. Would that be to your liking?"

"Yes," she said, her voice breathy. "Very much so."

Although she was starting to melt in response to his touch, there was still some tension there. She wasn't yet fully relaxed, or at least not as much as he wished. Leaning in, he kissed the edge of her jaw while drawing slow circles against her thigh with his thumb.

Her arm came around him, bringing him closer. The scratch of her nails against his scalp as her nails raked his hair, threatened to set him on fire. He curled his fingers around her inner thigh and smiled with smug satisfaction when she repositioned herself to grant him more access.

Distraction had helped her abandon her inhibitions, turning her into the wanton he'd first glimpsed at Seaton Hall and later today, in the carriage. He loved her that way – wild and free and ready to get up to all sorts of mischief.

Kissing her deeply, he gave her what she desired, bringing her right to the edge of the cliff before pulling her back.

"Callum," she muttered in utter frustration. "You can't just…"

Rather than answer, he kissed his way down her throat while undoing the fastenings on her gown. The decolletage dipped to reveal the perfect swell of her breasts and Callum's pulse spiked. Crushing her mouth with his, he took her on a sensual journey that saw his jacket and waistcoat removed, his shirt untucked, her bodice pulled down to her waist, and her skirts pushed up to her knees.

Her questing fingers dipped into his waistband while he worked on ridding her of her stay.

"You're so bloody gorgeous," he whispered as soon as the item had been removed. Hovering over her while she leaned back, he gazed into her yearning eyes. The hunger he saw there matched his own. "We probably ought to retreat upstairs."

"Must we?"

Callum's heart raced. "You don't mind doing it here?"

"We're alone, are we not, with no risk of discovery?"

"Yes." His muscles flexed with desire.

"A rare occasion, I suspect." Those eager fingers of hers found their way to his placket. "Besides, I'm not sure I have the patience required to wait until—"

Callum's mouth was upon hers again. Hell, she didn't need to convince him that they were in the perfect place for their coupling. He'd only wanted her to be more comfortable, but if she liked this, if she enjoyed having him on the sofa, then who was he to complain?

Instead, he pushed her skirts up even farther, undid his placket, and found the place where he'd always belonged.

Ensuring she received the caresses she needed, he brought her back to the edge of the cliff with stunning swiftness.

Gasping, she clutched at his shoulders while his every movement grew more erratic. Blood pounded through him. His stomach tightened. Hot little shivers raced down his spine, propelling him forward until he finally found the pleasure he sought in her arms.

A guttural moan assured him she accompanied

him off the cliff, flying beside him while stars burst around them.

The experience was, he later reflected, the most incredible and unifying one of his life. It bound him to Emily in a way nothing else could, aligning their bodies and minds, and making them one.

"I love you," he told her as soon as he'd caught his breath. Having moved slightly sideways, he supported most of his weight on his forearm so he wouldn't crush her.

Her fingers trailed up and down the length of his spine. "I love you too, Callum. Enormously much."

Sensing there was something else she wanted to say, he lifted his head and noted that her expression had grown a bit pensive. "What is it?"

She instantly blushed and gave him a hesitant look. "I was merely thinking of that thing you mentioned at Seaton Hall. Do you suppose we might try it tonight?"

He had no trouble recalling what she referred to. To his dismay, the suggestive idea immediately had him ready for additional bed sport. "That and lots of other things. First, however, I think we should both divest of the rest of our clothes. I for one, am rather eager to see you completely naked."

"I'm eager to see you as well," she confessed, the softness in her voice suggesting a hint of shyness that hadn't been there a second ago. It was returning now that their moment of wild abandon had passed.

In time, Callum hoped it would disappear fully. For now, he understood that the simplest way to beat it was through the art of seduction. And since they had an entire night, he intended to take his time.

With this in mind, he gathered his wife in his arms and stood. "I think it's time for you to become acquainted with our bedchamber."

"And for me to do that thing I promised."

He growled as he remembered what she referred to. He'd dreamed of it every night since. So, he hastened his step and climbed the stairs, happy and content in the knowledge that he had found the perfect partner in the most unlikely candidate he'd have imagined. And he intended to guard her and keep her until his dying breath.

EPILOGUE

London, 1834

Emily grabbed her shawl as she left the bedchamber she and her husband had shared for the past seventeen years. Halting at the next bedchamber door, she gave it a knock and entered.

"Are you ready to leave?" she asked.

Two young women, one of debutante age, the other a little bit younger, faced her with eager expressions.

"Yes, Mama," said Margaret. As the eldest, she was expected to make her debut later that evening. But before that happened, she and her sister would join their parents for a more public event.

"Emily," Callum called from the foyer, in what

most people would likely consider a very uncouth manner. "We have to go."

"We're coming, Papa," shouted Elizabeth, the youngest of the two sisters.

Emily chuckled and sent her daughters a let's-go look before leaving their room. Confident they would hurry as much as they could, she descended the stairs to the foyer where Callum stood waiting. He greeted her with a wide smile, which was quickly followed by a passionate kiss, despite their butler's presence.

Their daughters soon joined them and the family departed.

Although *Seductive Scandal* still didn't bear the names of those who'd written it, the subsequent books did. They referenced The Gentlemen Authors beneath the titles, with a brief biography of each man as part of the small introduction that preceded every story. Of which there were now ten in total.

The number of people who came to have their books signed by the dukes never ceased to amaze Emily. Today would be no different, she realized, when their carriage pulled to a halt in front of Between the Pages. Dozens of customers, women and men included, lined the pavement in anticipation of Callum's, Anthony's, and Brody's arrivals.

"I wager there are more people here to see Papa than what I'll encounter tonight at the ball," Margaret said, her voice filled with awe.

"Your papa and his friends are immensely popular," Emily agreed. She squeezed Callum's hand and leaned in to give him a kiss on the cheek. "I couldn't be prouder."

"And to think it all started here," he said with a nod toward the bookshop. "Seems like a lifetime ago, yet almost as though it were just yesterday."

Emily agreed. It was often difficult for her to fathom how long it had been since she and Callum had married. She waited for him and their daughters to alight before letting him help her down. So much had happened during the intervening years, not just for them, but for their friends too.

Ada and Anthony's marriage had been extremely productive. They now had four sons and three daughters between the ages of three and sixteen. Since Ada's uncle was no longer able to run Between the Pages, Ada had hired a clerk and a bookbinder to do so in his stead. Covering the extra expense had not been a problem. Much like Callum, Anthony and Brody had both invested the earnings they'd made on the first few books they'd sold, allowing all three to rebuild their fortunes.

Despite being financially stable, however, Harriet remained in Hudson & Co.'s employ since she loved her job there as a compositor far too much to give it up. Having purchased the business from Mr. Hudson when he retired a few years ago, Brody worked alongside his wife, making sure every book The

Gentlemen Authors published, was up to par. And with a few extra people in their employ, the Duke and Duchess of Corwin made sure to make time for their three sons as well.

Emily and Callum crossed the street with their daughters and greeted the customers who waited outside before entering the shop, which was already packed with people. Ushering Margaret and Elizabeth forward, between herself and Callum, Emily followed them through the crowd and toward the counter where Anthony and Brody waited together with Ada and Harriet.

"This looks like the best turnout yet," Callum said once they'd greeted their friends. "I'm rather impressed."

"And to think we're ten minutes early," Emily said as she scanned the full space.

"We were actually hoping there might be time for a toast before getting started," Ada said. "Anthony brought champagne."

"I think that will have to wait," Harriet said while glancing toward the front of the shop. "We'll celebrate later."

"Perhaps with the rest of the family," Anthony suggested.

Brody raised an eyebrow. "Everyone included?"

"Perhaps not everyone," Anthony said as he drew Ada into a sideways embrace. "Our youngest will have to stay home. But, we could ask Finn and Penny to join us."

Brody's troublemaker of a brother, Finnegan Evans, Marquess of Losturn, had fallen madly in love with Anthony's sister, Penelope, after dancing with her at her debut. She'd welcomed his courtship, but had turned down his offers of marriage until he'd convinced her that he'd reformed and had what it took to support a family. Desperate to prove himself worthy, he'd followed his older brother's example by selling off several possessions and investing his funds.

The returns had been used to open a winery, which had since become a lucrative business.

"It can't be tonight I'm afraid," said Callum. "Margaret is being presented at court at four o'clock, after which she's due to attend her debutant ball."

"Do you think Peter will make it home in time?" Margaret asked Emily with a hint of anxiousness in her voice.

"He said he would, so I'm certain he shall," Emily assured her. After acquiring a law degree from Oxford University, Peter had become an exceptionally good solicitor. The only trouble was, he'd chosen to work in Manchester, so Emily and Callum rarely saw him.

Emily studied Margaret, noted the relief in her eyes, and wondered if she might have developed a tendre for the young man. Emily's lips twitched with amusement. Wouldn't that be something?

"What is it?" Callum asked.

She caught his gaze. "Nothing. I'll tell you later."

"If you're ready," Ada said, "I would suggest we get started. If there's time once we finish, we'll pop the champagne for a quick toast before Callum and Emily have to leave. We can have a bigger celebration tomorrow."

The three men took their positions at the counter, their quills at the ready. Emily gestured for the first customer to step forward, then watched with delight as Callum signed his name to the title page of his latest release.

Her gaze met Ada's and Harriet's, and their answering smiles informed her that no matter how much time passed or how many books their husbands released, they would always be equally proud. These were the men they'd fallen in love with. Some might say the matches, which required overcoming class differences, mistaken identities, and misunderstandings, were most unlikely.

In Emily's opinion, they were perfect in their uniqueness. She, for one, was immensely happy, and when she caught Callum's gaze moments later and he smiled at her with love in his eyes, she had no doubt he felt the same way.

Thank you so much for taking the time to read A Duke's Lesson in Charm, the final book in my Gentlemen Authors series. If you enjoyed this story, you'll also enjoy The Brazen Beauties, starting with Mr. Dale and the Divorcée, an enemies to lovers romance.

You can find out more about my new releases, backlist deals and giveaways by signing up for my newsletter here: www.sophiebarnes.com

Follow me on Facebook for even more updates and join Sophie Barnes' Historical Romance Group for fun book related posts, games, discussions, and giveaways.

Once again, I thank you for your interest in my books. Please take a moment to leave a review since this can help other readers discover stories they'll love. And please continue reading for an excerpt from **Mr. Dale and the Divorcée.**

Keep reading for an excerpt from
Mr. Dale and The Divorcée
A Brazen Beauties novel

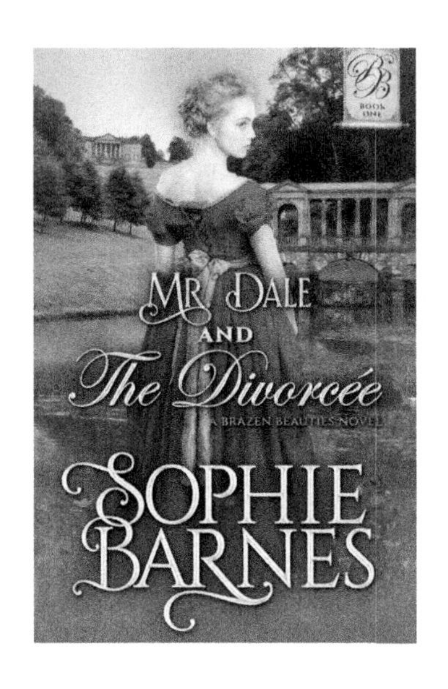

CHAPTER ONE

London, 1818

It was horribly hard for Wilhelmina Hewitt to find the words she needed to start this discussion. But after all her husband, George, had done for her, she felt it her duty now to help him as best she could. Even if the subject she wished to broach would probably shock him.

"Would you like a brandy?" he offered, the gentle sound of his voice conveying the warmth and consideration he'd always shown her.

Her resolve – the complete lack of nervousness she experienced in spite of her decision – surprised Wilhelmina. Instead of panic, an extraordinary sense of calm overcame her. She knew she was making the right choice, no matter how much it was destined to upend her life.

She considered her husband with deliberate practicality. The man she'd married twenty years earlier when she'd been eighteen and pregnant reclined in the armchair opposite hers, his gaze expectant. Their fathers had been like brothers.

They'd attended the same schools, had fought side by side in the American War of Independence, and had later perished together at sea.

Wilhelmina and George had both been ten years old when news of their fathers' deaths had arrived. With their properties less than one mile apart, they'd quickly found solace in each other. As one would expect, the incident had deepened the bond they'd already shared since birth. So when Wilhelmina faced the greatest ordeal of her life eight years later, George hadn't hesitated for a second. Having recently been denied the woman he loved, he'd insisted he'd never want to wed another. So he'd chosen to protect Wilhelmina instead. George had, she acknowledged, sacrificed more for her than what was fair. It was time she returned the favor.

Deciding to be direct, she cleared her throat. "I think we ought to get a divorce."

George's eyes widened. He stared at her as if she were mad. "I beg your pardon?"

Wilhelmina took a deep breath. "How long have you and Fiona been seeing each other?"

His gaze slid away from hers as his cheeks grew ruddy. "You know the answer to that."

"By my estimation it's almost exactly two years. Two years of pretending Fiona is my dearest friend – that it is me she comes to see thrice a week, not you." The lovely widow, ten years George's junior, had caught his attention one evening at Almack's.

The two had struck up a conversation, which had led to a dance. When subsequent run-ins with Fiona had increased George's interest in her, Wilhelmina had decided to step in and help the pair. By covering for them, she'd allowed them to conduct their affair in private and without scrutiny.

It was, she realized, an unconventional arrangement. But then again, her entire marriage was far from ordinary. The one and only attempt she and George had made to consummate their union turned out to be a spectacular failure. Bedding each other had been impossible due to their being like brother and sister and, Wilhelmina admitted, due to her own aversion for the act itself. So she'd happily encouraged George to pursue such relationships elsewhere in the years since.

"I'm sorry. I did not realize you were opposed to our meetings. You never—"

"George." Wilhelmina gave her husband a reassuring smile. "I believe you've misunderstood my reason for suggesting a divorce. It is not because I'm offended or upset by the relationship you and Fiona enjoy, but rather because I believe you have fallen in love with her and she with you."

He sat utterly motionless for a moment, then finally nodded. They'd always been frank with each other. "You're correct, but divorce is not the answer, Mina. It would be public and messy. Our reputations would be destroyed in the process – yours especially."

Bolstering herself against the truth of his words, she shrugged one shoulder. "I'll manage."

"No." He shook his head. "I won't have that on my conscience."

She stood and went to crouch before him. Her hand clasped his. A pair of dark brown eyes filled with concern met hers. "You gave up on love for me once – on starting a family of your own. Please, allow me to return the enormous favor you did me when you decided to save me from ruin and Cynthia from illegitimacy."

"Ah, but I did marry for love, Mina."

"I know, but not in the way you should have."

"If you think I have regrets, you're wrong. I'd make the same decision again in a heartbeat."

"Because you're the best man there is, George. And as such, you deserve every happiness in the world. You deserve to have a life with Fiona just as she deserves to have a life with you." She carefully released his hand, then stood and crossed to the sideboard where she proceeded to fill two glasses with brandy. Returning, she handed him his drink and took a sip of her own.

A frown appeared on George's brow. "You've no idea how hard it would be to break up our marriage completely. We're not just speaking of legal separation, Mina, which in and of itself is enough to see one shunned from Society. What you're suggesting would require parliamentary involvement with three readings of the divorcement bill before the Lords. Witnesses to your adulterous behavior would have to give evidence."

"I've thought about that. Obviously, the simplest thing to do would be to pay a few men for the trouble."

He gaped at her, then took a sip of his drink. "No. I appreciate the offer, but we'll do no such thing."

"George. I really—"

"It's absolutely out of the question."

"You're certain I can't persuade you?"

He gave her a steady look. "Quite."

"All right," Mina agreed after a moment's hesitation. She knew when George was beyond budging. "But this arrangement with Fiona is untenable. It's just a matter of time before someone catches on to the fact that the two of you are lovers, and when they do, she will suffer the most. So if you refuse a divorce, you should at the very least consider moving out of Town. Find a small village somewhere so you can carry on with each other discreetly."

"And leave you here by yourself? Would that not raise a few eyebrows?"

"Not if you come back from time to time and visit. Plenty of husbands travel for work."

"My work, as you well know, is here in London."

"It doesn't have to be." As the designer and manufacturer of fine furniture, George had made a name for himself amid the upper class. Having a Hewitt sofa was all the rage. So much so they'd both been admitted into upper class circles and counted Viscount and Viscountess Pennington among their dearest friends. "You already have employees who are trained to handle new orders along with the shop on a regular basis. Whether you sit in your study here and create new designs or you do so a hundred miles away would make little difference, would it not?"

"I suppose not."

"Especially if you were to set up a home near Croft, which in my mind would make your life simpler since that's where the carpenters are."

For the first time since this conversation had begun, George allowed a hint of humor to tug at his lips. "You've put a frightening amount of thought into this. If I didn't know any better, I'd think you were eager to be rid of me."

"Not at all," she told him in earnest. "I merely desire to see you happy."

He seemed to mull this over a moment. "I'll think on it. Right now, there's still Cynthia's upcoming wedding to consider. Moving ahead with any drastic changes should probably wait until she has spoken her vows. I'd hate to give Mr. Petersen or his parents a reason to call things off."

"Agreed."

George finally smiled. "Good. That's settled then. Care for a game of cards?"

Wilhelmina located the deck and returned to her seat. She knew George was being protective. It was in his nature. But she hated feeling like she was becoming a hindrance to him, a burden keeping him from the life he deserved.

Of course, altering his perspective only required a change in circumstance. This was apparent when he came to speak with Wilhelmina six months later. In the sort of bleak tone one might use when there'd been a death in the family, he announced that he'd gotten Fiona with child.

"I'm sorry," he muttered. Slumped in the same chair he'd used for their previous conversation on the matter, he clasped his head between his hands. No man had ever looked more defeated or miserable. It broke Wilhelmina's heart. The joy George would surely have felt over the pregnancy was being overshadowed by the complication of his marriage to her.

Now, faced with a choice between the scandal of divorce or bringing an illegitimate child into the world, she knew his hand had been forced by fate. As such, the only thing she could think to do was offer comfort and reassurance as he'd so often done for her. "It's all right. I will survive this, George. We all will."

"I've spoken about it at length with Fiona. She

asked me to convey her gratitude. What you are willing to do is—"

"The correct thing."

"Mina..." His voice was thick with feeling.

"Moving forward, we'll need a plan," she told him matter-of-factly before she too succumbed to emotion. "Right now, only the three of us know the true nature of this marriage or that you and I share a bond stronger than what most married couples enjoy. If we are to succeed in dissolving our marriage completely, we'll need to put up a good façade. The fewer people we confide in, the better."

"I've considered this too," George said. "I think we need to tell Cynthia and her husband, Henry, what to expect. I also think it would benefit you if one or two of our closest friends, like the Penningtons, were brought into our confidence. This way, you won't be completely alone afterward."

"Maybe," she agreed. "From what I gather, you and I shan't be permitted to see each other once the divorce has been settled."

"Not that we'd have much opportunity to." When she gave him a puzzled look he explained, "Although getting through this may take a long time, Fiona and I intend to leave England as soon as it's over since staying here and facing the aftermath could be difficult for our child."

Wilhelmina's stomach clenched at the idea of George moving overseas. He'd always been there and while she was happy to help him marry Fiona, she instantly knew his absence from England would lead to an unwelcome emptiness in her heart. For his sake, she forced herself to maintain her composure.

"Where will you go?"

"Massachusetts has a well-established logging industry, but it's my understanding that the area surrounding the Great Lakes shows promise. It's reputed to be an especially stunning part of North America. Most importantly, it's far away."

It certainly was. Wilhelmina forced a smile and tried not to panic. This was for the best. George would be with the woman he loved and start a family. With Cynthia already settled a few months earlier, her future had been secured. As for Wilhelmina herself, she'd weather the storm as best as she could, most likely by focusing all her energy on the property she owned near Renwick. George had helped her purchase the small farm nearly five years ago. After a serious bout of influenza, he'd insisted on making sure she'd have a property in her own name in case he died. She'd not been there often, but having it did reassure her.

"You do realize your child will likely be born out of wedlock," Wilhelmina said. She hated bringing this up, but decided it was best to face the facts, no matter how unappealing. "From what I gather, the proceedings we intend to undertake could last a couple of years."

George's gaze finally sharpened. "I'm aware, but once it's done, my son or daughter shall have my name."

Wilhelmina nodded. "With this in mind, let's get to work on ruining my reputation."

ACKNOWLEDGMENTS

I would like to thank the Killion Group for their incredible help with the editing and cover design for this book.

And to my friends and family, thank you for your constant support and for believing in me. I would be lost without you!

ABOUT THE AUTHOR

USA TODAY bestselling author Sophie Barnes is best known for her historical romance novels in which the characters break away from social expectations in their quest for happiness and love. Having written for Avon, an imprint of Harper Collins, her books have been published internationally in eight languages.

With a fondness for travel, Sophie has lived in six countries, on three continents, and speaks English, Danish, French, Spanish, and Romanian with varying degrees of fluency. Ever the romantic, she married the same man three times—in three different countries and in three different dresses.

When she's not busy dreaming up her next swoon worthy romance novel, Sophie enjoys spending time with her family, practicing yoga, baking, gardening, watching romantic comedies and, of course, reading.

You can contact her through her website at www.sophiebarnes.com

For all the latest releases, promotions, and exclusive story updates, subscribe to Sophie Barnes' newsletter today!

And please consider leaving a review for this book.

Every review is greatly appreciated!

Printed in Great Britain
by Amazon